Emily FoR Real

Emily FoR Real

Sylvia Gunnery

pajamapress

The publisher gratefully acknowledges the support of the Canada Council for the
Arts and the Ontario Arts Council for its publishing program. We acknowledge
the financial support of the Government of Canada through the Book Publishing
Industry Development Program (BPIDP) for our publishing activities.

Library and Archives Canada Cataloguing in Publication

Gunnery, Sylvia

    Emily for real / Sylvia Gunnery.

ISBN 978-0-9869495-8-6

    I. Title.

PS8563.U575E55 2012   jC813'.54   C2012-900417-0

U.S. Publisher Cataloging-in-Publication Data (U.S.)

Gunnery, Sylvia, 1946-
    Emily for real / Sylvia Gunnery.
[ ] p. : cm.
Summary: Seventeen-year old Emily's world crumbles when her boyfriend dumps
her, and, when she thinks her life can't possibly get any worse, a series of secrets are
revealed that threaten to tear her beloved family apart. Emily feels like she has no
one to turn to, until an unexpected friendship blossoms with a troubled classmate
name Leo. Sometimes despondent, but always supportive, Leo is Emily's rock in an
ocean of confusion and disbelief.
ISBN-13: 978-0-98694-958-6 (pbk.)
1. Friendship – Juvenile fiction. 2. Adoption – Juvenile fiction. 3. Coming of age –
Juvenile fiction.
[Fic] dc23   PZ7.G8664em 2012

Book and cover design–Rebecca Buchanan
Photography–James Bell
Manufactured by Webcom. Printed in Canada.

MIX
Paper from
responsible sources
FSC® C004071

Pajama Press Inc.
469 Richmond St E, Toronto Ontario, Canada
www.pajamapress.ca

For Jim

Acknowledgments

I acknowledge, with much appreciation, the opportunity to dedicate time to this book in its early stages during my three months as writer-in-residence with the Nova Scotia South Shore Public Libraries. I also thank the Canada Council for the Arts and the Writers' Federation of Nova Scotia for their support.

Throughout the development of Emily's story, I was encouraged by students in Bob Hazelton and Paula Munro's English 10 Plus classes at Forest Heights Community School in Chester Basin, Nova Scotia. I thank them for believing in Emily and Leo, as well as for sharing their own fictions in our writing workshops.

I thank Theo who walked into my high school English class several years ago, criticized Shakespeare as being "a pervert," soon became my friend, and then stayed on in my imagination as Leo in this novel.

Gail Winskill took my manuscript and quickly moved it along the path to publication, all the while asking the right questions, offering precise and valuable comments…and listening. Thank you, Gail.

… I've spent summers watching satellites
thinking they were stars and who
knows what it is you are.

—Sue Goyette, "So Quite New"

One

I suddenly know exactly what I have to do. It's more like an impulse than a plan because right now my brain's on shutdown. I go to the bottom drawer of my desk and dig out my photo album that's mostly filled with pictures of Brian and me. I pick up the scissors and take everything over to my bed. My heart's squeezed tight and I'm shaking inside.

Then I start. Page by page, picture by picture, I remove any ones that have Brian in them. If it's just him, I cut a clean diagonal right across the middle, letting one half fall dead on the bed and throwing the other half on top of the pile. If it's a picture of him with me, I carefully slice him off, and for some reason I save the piece with me in it.

After a while, there's a pile of Brian corpses lying there staring at nothing, and the pages of my album are all patched up with slices and triangles and scraps of pictures of me. In every one of these sliced-up pictures, I look stranded. Like there was an earthquake and I'm left on the edge of some kind of half-destroyed world.

Instead of feeling better, I feel worse. Like I'm not really me anymore. I don't feel like crying. I don't feel like anything.

I know I'll have to get rid of the sliced-up pictures of Brian before anyone sees them and has a chance to know how truly crazed I am.

People think I'm depressed because of Granddad. I'm not. Today was his funeral, but I wasn't close to Granddad even though I'm his only grandchild. You know how some grandfathers sit in big chairs and read you stories while you stare at the pictures and suck your thumb, or how they let you comb their hair, even if there's not much hair to comb? Granddad is a different species than that. Was.

If this was a movie about me and it was the opening scene, a funeral would be perfect. The funeral of my relationship with Brian.

Brian's at McGill University and already he has this French girlfriend. Six weeks in Montreal and he has this French girlfriend. If he'd texted me, I could have read it over and over and maybe read between the lines. But he called and said he wanted to tell me because I deserved to know and he was sorry.

Then Granddad had a heart attack and died watching golf on TV, so I haven't told anyone about Brian. And I already know that life has its ups and downs, that there's more fish in the sea, that love can be cruel, and any other cliché that's supposed to make you feel good but only makes you want to puke.

Dad and Aunt Em are having a reception-slash-party so people can pay their respects to Granddad. Meredith would've been the only one who really had any respects to pay, but she doesn't actually remember that she was married to him. When we went to the nursing home so Dad could tell her that Granddad died, all she said was, "Is it raining out?" Then she said to me, "Emma, go look and see if it's raining."

I don't mind when she calls me Emma. She's not confused saying Aunt Em's name instead of mine. She actually thinks I am Aunt Em. Dad says Meredith loves them both as much as any mother would love her own children. I believe him.

I always knew how my Grandmother Rita died. No one told me about it, like, *Come here, Emily, sit down and I'll tell you what happened the day your grandmother died.* But Dad and Aunt Em talk about it a lot, even

3

though they were only five when it happened. They don't remember much, except about how sunny and warm it was for January and how she was alone in the car and how the car smashed into one of those supports for the overpass. When they got home from school for lunch, she wasn't there. The accident was happening around the time they were knocking on the door and shouting, "Mom! Mom!" over and over and wondering where she was. Ironic.

Granddad married Meredith just before Christmas that year. Lots of times Dad says to Mom that who could blame him with two five-year-old kids to look after.

And then Mom says, "Couldn't be responsible for you and your sister for even a year without finding a woman to do the job for him." It's no secret that Mom doesn't like Granddad much. Didn't like.

I'm standing here at the front door looking out through the screen, thinking about how normal a day seems to be when actually nothing's normal at all.

A taxi stops and a woman is in the back alone. She looks pretty old. The cab driver helps her out of the car.

She smiles when she gets close to me and says, "Oh, you must be Emily. Your grandfather told me all about you."

"You know Granddad?" *Knew.*

"Oh, yes."

When she's all the way into the front hall, Dad

comes out of the living room and I can see right away that he doesn't know who she is. He gets this half-smile on his face like he thinks he's supposed to know her.

"And you're Gerald," she says. "One of the twins."

I almost say she must be writing a book about our family. But like lots of things I almost blurt out, I manage not to.

Dad's forehead is crinkling up and I can tell he still has no clue who this person is.

"I'm Cynthia Maxwell," she says and shakes Dad's hand. "I'm a friend of your father's. I worked in Karl's office in that small house on Maple Street. That was years ago, of course. Before the new building on Victoria Street."

Dad's still drawing a blank.

"My husband and I moved to Montreal," she says. *Montreal.* "But Karl and I have kept in touch over the years. Karl was always very thoughtful. Very reliable."

I'm thinking, *Wrong Karl, wrong funeral.*

"Please come in Mrs. Maxwell," says Dad. "Emily, go tell Aunt Em that Mrs. Maxwell is here."

Can't wait to see Aunt Em draw a twin blank.

So finally Mrs. Maxwell's in a chair and she has a cup of tea with a small plate of sandwiches. I sit down by her while Dad and Aunt Em walk around, making sure everyone has coffee or tea. Mom's refilling plates with sandwiches or squares, rearranging stuff so the plates don't look so picked over.

Dad and Aunt Em don't know what to make of her. That's what Aunt Em will say when they're talking after this reception is over: *I don't know what to make of her.*

Cynthia Maxwell is telling me I have Dad's eyes and cheekbones. Dad doesn't really have cheekbones anymore but they're in pictures of him from twenty years ago. Everyone says I have Dad's eyes and cheekbones.

"Did you know my grandmother?" I ask. "Rita?"

"Yes," she says.

"For some reason, I've been thinking about her today, even though I never met her because she died years and years before I was even born. Granddad must have gone into shock when she died like that." But I don't say, that as far as I could see, he stayed in shock all his life because he sure didn't talk about Rita, and he sure didn't act like much of a father or grandfather.

"It was a terrible thing to bear," she says. "Life can be cruel."

Brian.

"But there are things we can't change and that we have to accept."

French girlfriend. "Would you like more tea?"

"No, thank you, dear."

"Sandwiches?"

"I've had plenty."

"Sweets?"

"No. No sweets. I have to watch the sweets."

And I see her watching sweets. Staring at a huge plate of them in her kitchen, wherever she lives. There are so many sweets on the plate they're stacked high and some are falling off. I'm losing my mind.

"There's something I've always wondered about when my Grandmother Rita died," I say.

She looks at me like I'm going to reveal the most important revelation.

"How come she was driving that far from the city when she knew Dad and Aunt Em would be coming home from school for lunch, and she was supposed to be home when they got there?"

"Yes," she says.

"I've always wondered that."

Her sandwiches are gone and her teacup is empty. She just sits there.

So I say, "But I never asked anyone about that because I thought it would hurt their feelings. Because she wasn't home when she was supposed to be looking after her children."

"It was a long time ago."

And I can't tell if that means she couldn't remember anything about the accident, or whether it didn't much matter anyway because Rita is dead and now Grand-dad is dead and probably she's thinking her turn's next. Dad said to Aunt Em the day Granddad died, "We're orphans now, Emma."

Mrs. Maxwell doesn't stay very long. It's strange that she didn't ask any questions about our family. But like she said, she and Granddad kept in touch over the years so she probably already knew everything.

"What do you make of her?" Aunt Em's washing cups and saucers and Dad's drying them. Mom's gone to lie down now that the reception is finally over. I'm arranging leftover sandwiches and squares and cookies in plastic containers, thinking I don't want to take any of this stuff to school for lunch. Not because it was funeral food. Anything leftover should have a salmonella sign stamped on it.

"Seems nice enough," says Dad.

Aunt Em says, "I don't remember Dad ever talking about a Cynthia Maxwell, do you?"

"No."

"Granddad didn't talk about anyone he used to know," I say a bit sarcastically.

"That's not true. He talked about lots of people from his past."

"But no Cynthia Maxwell or Mr. Maxwell," I say, like I have a point to prove. Dad just gives me a look and I realize I'm talking like this because I'm getting frustrated with this whole Brian-death-funeral-reception week. "Maybe Meredith knows her," I say as a peace offering. Sometimes if you say a name, Meredith connects the dots.

"Time to head on home," says Aunt Em.

"It's been an emotional four days," says Dad.

We're orphans now, Emma.

Aunt Em hangs the wet dish towel on the oven door. "Be nice to be home and put my feet up." And have a smoke, she doesn't say. "Blanche is probably meowing at her empty dish."

Then she comes over and gives me her usual kiss on the cheek, and I give her a hug, thinking I'd like to tell her about Brian, but it isn't really the right time and place, as Mom would say.

After she leaves I go to my room and listen to music and picture Brian talking slow French to this girl in *Montreal* and her giggling when his accent sounds English and his smile and brown eyes and just the way he tilts his head sideways when he's kissing. His soft soft lips and how sweet his breath smells. The pressure of his mouth and how he sometimes moans and pulls me in closer, tighter.

But it's not me. It's her.

Crying is not cathartic.

Two

Jenn has her own car. Her father sold it to her for one hundred dollars a month, which she pays out of money from her job at the mall. It'll take her two years to pay for it, but it's still a good deal. And she gets 20 percent off clothes where she works.

Sometimes my mind swims with details like how much Jenn pays for her car and what percent she gets off clothes. I don't really plan to think about stuff like that, it just happens. Even if I look up at this tree and try to concentrate on how beautiful the sun is, shining through those yellow leaves, hundreds of yellow leaves like a brilliant tent over my head, I end up back where I was, thinking about one hundred dollars a month times two years equals $2400, which is a good deal for a car. And I'm thinking all this while I'm waiting for Jenn to pick me up for school.

"You do the math homework?" I ask, even though I already know the answer. Jenn finds school so easy, partly because she does all the work and partly because she's just brilliant. In grade two she got in trouble for reading a book upside down. The teacher thought she was being a smart-ass (not that she'd ever say it that way), but Jenn was just bored. After that I tried reading upside down. It's not easy.

"You won't get in trouble for not doing the math," she says. "They know about your grandfather, don't they?"

"I don't want any sympathetic looks. Pathetic looks."

Jenn laughs and gives me her best pathetic look. Then she says, "Linda's having a party Friday. Ronny'll be there."

"What's that got to do with anything?"

"Come on, Em."

"Come on what?"

She looks at me sideways for a nanosecond because she has to keep her eyes on the road. The look means that she knows that I know what she's talking about.

But I fake that I don't get it. "What?"

"I refuse to state the obvious."

"Well, I don't get the obvious, then."

"You can't tell me Ronny's not hot. You even thought he was hot in grade four."

"Okay, so Ronny's hot. So what?"

She turns into the school parking lot and concentrates on squeezing in between two cars. Then she switches off the engine, checks her teeth in the mirror, and runs her fingers through her bangs to mess them up. "It's not like Brian's the only male on this planet," she says. "You haven't seen him for almost two months and then he calls you up and dumps you. Come on, Em. Forget Brian. Ronny's your *target*."

Jenn's like that. Practical. When one situation's over, move on. She's left a lot of romantic wreckage behind her and didn't even hear the last tinkle of glass falling. She has her pick of any guy she wants. It's because of her looks: short brown hair, green eyes, small nose, big lips, small body, big breasts, white teeth, big smile. I could go on. *Target*, she says, because she has the power to aim.

"I don't want a target."

"Yes, you do. Hey, there's Ronny."

"If you say anything that even—"

"Hi, Ronny. Going to Linda's on Friday?"

Ronny's not looking at any of the bigs and smalls and whites of Jenn. He's looking at me. "You guys going?"

"Sure," says Jenn. She's smiling because she can see Ronny's looking at me.

This reminds me of how I've been feeling ever since Brian left for Montreal. Just because he's not in the picture anymore, guys suddenly notice I exist. Like I'm some kind of manikin on display and everyone's window-shopping.

"See you there, then," he says, and catches up to the guys he was with.

"Hot Ronny has the hots for you," says Jenn with this silly grin and with her eyes blinking like flashbulbs are going off in front of her face.

"Don't exaggerate," I say and she smirks.

After school I get it into my head to go see Meredith, which I've never done without Mom or Dad or Aunt Em. I want to ask her about Cynthia Maxwell, like I'm some kind of detective. I don't know why my brain's so fixated on this but it is. Maybe it's tired of being so fixated on Brian Brian Brian. Desperate for a diversion. Any diversion.

Jenn drives me to the nursing home, which is a big favor because it's halfway across the city. Harmony Hills isn't actually built on hills. There's only one floor, with two long corridors that meet in the middle where there's a big TV room with huge sofas and chairs that are usually empty. That's on one side of the hall, and on the other is a dining room that has tables with paper flowers in skinny vases. For Meredith (I've always called her Meredith because Mom and Dad and Aunt Em always call her that) life centers on going to that dining room three times a day. She has to walk with a walker but she can still feed herself.

"Hi, Meredith," I say as I walk into her small room. She shares this room with Rose, who sleeps almost all the time in her chair by the window, like she's doing right now.

Meredith looks up at me from her own comfy chair. I think she's wondering who I am.

"Oh, look!" I say like it's a big surprise. "The flowers Dad brought the other day aren't wilted!" I'm thinking about how wilted everyone in this place is and maybe that's not such a great word to use under the circumstances. "They're beautiful! Pink! Your favorite color!" Even with all these exclamations, Meredith is just staring at me like I'm a TV.

One of the personal care workers comes in, maybe because of all the shouting I'm doing. She's wearing a blue top that looks like pajamas with teddy bears all over it. Why do they have to wear stuff like that with teddy bears and fluffy ducks when there's no kids around?

"I see you have company, sweetheart," the care worker says to Meredith, gently touching her cheek. "Emily's here."

I'm embarrassed because she knows my name and I never can remember any of the care workers' names. But then I notice that this person has a heart-shaped pin that says *Lucy*. Good clue. I'm brilliant.

"How's your family getting along?" she asks, meaning how are we coping with the fact that my grandfather is dead.

"Pretty good," I say.

"Mr. Sinclair came to see Meredith every week. I think she misses him terribly."

I put on a fake smile. Who's she kidding? Meredith misses no one because she remembers no one. Hello! Which suddenly makes me feel totally stupid coming here to ask about Cynthia Maxwell. Who'm *I* kidding?

The care worker leaves and I sit on the edge of Meredith's bed next to her chair. I take her hand, partly to get her attention and partly because that's what Dad and Aunt Em do when they come to see her, like if she can't remember you, she can feel you. "We had a big reception for Granddad yesterday," I say. "Lots of people came to pay their respects."

"Oh?" She says this like she's not really interested, then looks down at our hands.

"And Cynthia came too. Cynthia Maxwell."

That name obviously doesn't ring a bell.

"Dad and Aunt Em said they didn't know who she

was but she said she worked at Granddad's office a long time ago before she moved away." I didn't say "to Montreal" because I don't like admitting that city exists.

Then Meredith looks at me and smiles. "I didn't expect you today," she says, but right away I know she doesn't mean that she actually knows I'm Emily and that this is Wednesday.

But I go with the flow. "Oh, I just thought I'd drop by after school. Boy, those teachers make us do so much lame stuff all day and then pile on more for homework." I laugh so she'll know I'm joking.

"Where's Gerald?"

"He's probably still at work." Then I humor myself and ask, "Do you remember anyone called Cynthia Maxwell who used to work with Granddad?"

When I get home, I probably won't tell Dad and Mom about visiting Meredith. I know they'll think it was a nice thing to do because there's Meredith, pretty much all by herself all day. But maybe they'll start to clue in that something about me has changed and I'll have to explain about Brian. That I don't need.

Linda's place is packed with mostly people I know, but there's a big gap in who's here compared to a few months ago, and it's not just Brian I'm talking about.

Tons of people aren't around anymore because of moving away to university or doing whatever else they're doing since graduating.

It's depressing.

Jenn hands me a beer and says, "Cheer up." She clinks the bottom of her bottle against the bottom of mine like we have a conspiracy. She looks around at people standing and sitting and dancing and getting beers and I know she's trying to figure out how to rearrange everybody so I'm drinking this beer next to Ronny.

Then Ronny comes over and stands beside me. Jenn has no idea the power she has.

"Hey, there's Greg!" she says with pseudo excitement because I know Greg's not high on her list. She leaves Ronny and me standing there alone. Surprise.

Ronny's already had too many beers. He's leaning toward me at a precarious angle.

"How'd you do that?" I ask, because he has a small gash on the back of the hand that's holding his beer.

"Playin' with our dog," he says. "I steal her fake bone and she goes nuts."

I picture him laughing and rolling around on a carpet with a sweet little puppy yapping and bounding and trying to get her fake bone back. My fake heart gets all soft because of what I'm picturing. I drink some more beer.

18

When the song changes, Ronny takes my hand and we move away from the wall and start dancing, still holding our beers. Mine is pressed against his chest and his is resting on my back. I like being inside the leather smell of his jacket and the beer smell and the darkness of the room with my eyes closed and our bodies moving together exactly the same. I'm pretending he's Brian.

That's what I'm remembering, lying here on my bed. My head is pounding. I tried to throw up a while ago, but all I did was just spit out this bubbly beige stuff. Toilets can make you feel ashamed when you're looking into them like that.

Jenn'll be pushing me for details.

Nothing happened, really.

At some point Ronny and I left Linda's party and went over to his house, which was not that far. We were laughing and walking down the street drinking beers, with my arm around his waist and his arm around my shoulder.

His room is in the basement and he has his own door at the back of the house. You go down a few steps to get to the door. I remember wondering where the dog was because there was no sound of any dog when we went into the house. His room has fake wood walls and a blue carpet and two small lamps with black shades. He has a water bed that he said belongs to his brother who's in the army. Just the way that bed rolled and sloshed when I sat down on it made me think of puking. I fell back and closed my eyes.

Ronny took off his jacket—I heard it drop on the floor. The bed rolled and sloshed again when he crawled in beside me.

When we were kissing, I couldn't concentrate on feeling anything. I forget if I said something. My mind was all over the place. His hair was against my mouth and his mouth was on my neck. He moved all the way on top of me and pulled at the zipper on my jeans. All I could think of was that this was a big mistake.

But the mistake didn't happen. Ronny passed out. It felt like he was dead. I pushed myself deeper into the water bed and rolled him off me. Then I hauled on my shoes and jacket and left.

Still no dog. Maybe there never was a dog.

"What?"

They're all looking at me and I can tell I've just caught them talking about something they don't want me to know about. I hate that. "What?" I say again.

Mom leaves the room.

Aunt Em looks at Dad. "She is seventeen, Gerry."

Dad looks at me as if he's trying to decide if I actually am seventeen.

"What?" I say again. Now I really have to know what's going on. In the back of my mind I'm thinking it has to do with Ronny and Friday night, but there's no way they could know about that. As if Ronny's going to call and say, *I think I had sex with Emily on Friday night but I can't remember much about it because I passed out.*

"But—," says Dad and looks at the doorway where Mom just made her exit.

Then I suddenly think that something's wrong with Mom and they don't want me to know. "Is something wrong with Mom?" I'm very worried and they can see it.

"Okay, tell her if you want," says Dad and he leaves the room too.

It can't be anything about Mom because of the way he said "if you want," like it's nothing that he has to tell me. It's a choice. Aunt Em's choice, for some reason.

I don't say *What?* again, but I'm thinking it.

Aunt Em looks at her hands spread on the kitchen table like someone's about to paint her fingernails. Then she looks at me. "You remember Cynthia Maxwell." It isn't a question, so I don't say anything. "Well, she phoned this morning. I was surprised she wasn't back in Montreal by now. Anyway, she invited me to tea at her hotel."

I just stand there because that bit of information sounds like only the beginning.

Aunt Em sighs and stops looking at her hands. "She told me she and Dad had an affair for twenty-three years. A relationship, she called it."

My brain just can't handle that information. Any of it. It's just too weird. Granddad and Cynthia Maxwell? Twenty-three years? Twenty-three!

"I agree," says Aunt Em, even though I haven't said anything. She read my face.

"That's too weird," is all I can manage to say. I don't like to think of my grandfather having sex so I'm blurring all the images that are trying to form in my mind. "And no one knew? What about Meredith?"

"We'll never know," she says, and I guess that's true.

"But Mrs. Maxwell lives in Montreal."

"Dad went to conferences all over the place. She went too."

I still can't picture this. "So why's she telling us now?"

"I think she needed us to know, to finally say that she used to be an important part of his life too. Knowing Dad, he would have insisted that she keep their secret. Not that it matters anymore."

Over my dead body, I hear him say. Then I think about Mom leaving the room like that and it makes sense. Just one more thing Granddad did to make her dislike him even more. If Mom had known about that affair, there would have been a million turkey dinners he would never have been invited to our house, that's for sure.

Then I think about how I might feel if Dad had an affair and I didn't know. "Are your feelings hurt?"

"Not really." But she sighs again, and when she looks up at me her face is all wobbly. "Emily," she says, "life isn't simple."

If I hadn't come into the kitchen like that just when they were talking about Cynthia Maxwell's secret life with Granddad, I don't think I'd know any of this stuff. So I say, "Brian broke up with me." I tell her this because I want her to know that I know life isn't simple.

Her face changes and I can see she's surprised. "When?"

"Last week. He has a new girlfriend. She's French and goes to McGill and I guess she's in one of his classes." I can't hold it in any longer and I start to cry.

Aunt Em gets up and gives me one of her hugs and smoothes my hair and says, "Emily, I'm sorry."

That's when Dad comes back into the room. "I can't believe he'd be that cold-hearted."

The room sort of changes temperature, like it feels colder and quieter.

"I didn't tell her everything," says Aunt Em softly. "Not about the accident."

Dad sits down. His shoulders cave in and he tells

me as much as he knows. "She drove over to Dad's office that morning and went up the outside back stairs to surprise him. She was bringing a picnic. She must've seen Dad and Cynthia Maxwell through the window. They found the picnic basket on the landing after Dad got the call that she wasn't home. Then the police came to say she died in the car accident." He hasn't looked at me the whole time he's telling this. "She was upset. Distracted."

"Gerry." Aunt Em is standing behind Dad with her hands on his shoulders.

"Jesus," he says.

"Twenty-three years," says Aunt Em in a whisper.

I'm thinking about Cynthia Maxwell getting married and moving to Montreal and Meredith marrying Granddad and loving Dad and Aunt Em as much as any mother would love her own children. And all those conferences where Cynthia Maxwell and Granddad had their affair.

But I'm quiet because now Dad and Aunt Em are looking at each other with nothing to say.

Three

Mr. Canning's writing on the board and doesn't notice there's a guy outside the door. The guy's big. Big. He isn't smiling and his black eyebrows have this permanent scowl. He's definitely not happy to be standing out there and it doesn't look like he'll be happy when he comes in.

Cory obviously knows him. "Hey, Leo. What's up?"

Mr. Canning looks over and sees the guy standing there. "Good morning," he says and walks to the door. "You must be Leo Mac. Welcome. Come in and find a seat. Perhaps—"

"He can sit here," says Cory, which surprises me because he's not exactly the welcoming-committee type. And *here* happens to be at this table where I'm sitting too.

Mr. Canning seems relieved that someone in the class knows Leo. "Excellent," he says. "Emily and Cory

can familiarize you with the assignment we've just begun."
He goes back to writing on the board while almost everyone else in the class is still checking out the new guy.

He walks over and sits down without saying anything. Then he notices the book next to my elbow and says, "*Romeo and Juliet*. What crap."

"It's not that bad." I'm a bit defensive because I've actually been liking *Romeo and Juliet*. Separated lovers. Dead-end romance. Story of my life.

"They're idiots," he says. "Do you know how old they are? She's twelve. Twelve! And Romeo's not much older. Shakespeare's a pervert."

Cory's enjoying this. He's leaning way back in his chair and grinning like it's a contest between this guy Leo and me, and I'm not winning.

I'm thinking about the look Cory'd have on his face if his chair slipped and he crashed to the floor.

"So you've already studied *Romeo and Juliet*," says Mr. Canning, who doesn't miss a thing even if his back is turned.

"Yeah. In grade five," says Leo with a smirk, exaggerating grade five.

"Shakespeare's writing appeals to all ages," says Mr. Canning. He puts down the chalk and comes to our table. "Since Nathaniel's absent this week, Cory and Emily could benefit from your help with their project, especially given your previous study of this Shakespearean tragedy."

Leo doesn't look interested in helping anyone. "I'm not acting anything out."

"You don't have to," says Cory. "We're supposed to come up with a theme song for act one, like if it's a movie. Then we have to explain why we picked it."

"Whoopee."

Already I like Leo. He's funny, if you look for it. He knows he's funny too because the corner of his mouth gets this little bend in it when he holds back a smile. Comic relief.

Jenn's waiting for me in the cafeteria. As if she'd eat. She only goes there because that's where everyone hangs out. She says it isn't attractive to have food in your mouth when you're checking guys out. She does have a point, but I'm starving. And I'm definitely not checking guys out. Indefinitely.

Cory and Leo and I are still together because the two of them are trying to convince me to lip-sync in English class tomorrow. They both play guitar and now they're suddenly into this project because they've got this idea to play along with the song we picked while I lip-sync.

"No way."

"Come on, Emily."

"No."

"What if we just do the last verse?" says Cory.

"That's the only one that's got anything to do with the stupid play, anyway," says Leo.

I can't believe he's even remotely interested in this project.

"We should practice," says Cory. "We could use our garage."

"Practice what?" says Jenn. She's looking at Leo, checking him out. He is definitely not her type. Too tall. Too big. Too interesting, actually.

"Good idea," says Leo. "What time?"

"I don't know. Seven? Eight?"

They both look at me.

"Count me out."

"Seven-thirty," says Leo. "See you later." And he leaves the cafeteria.

"Don't let us down, Emily," says Cory and he takes off too.

"Practice what?" says Jenn again.

"It's for English. And it's not gonna happen."

"Who's the new guy?"

"Leo. Cory knows him."

"Cory's cute."

"He has a girlfriend. Stop trying to set me up, Jenn."

"Don't blame me for Friday night."

I roll my eyes and go stand in line to get an egg sandwich on whole wheat. They're always the freshest.

It's 7:20. Every five minutes I'm looking at the clock and thinking there's no way I'm going over to Cory's to practice in his garage. But I'm lying to myself.

"I have to work on a project with a couple of guys in my English class," I say to Mom. "I'll just be over on Rosemead."

"Call Dad to come for you if it gets too late."

Mom's always picturing the worst-case scenario. She watches too much TV, like she's doing right now. She's happy watching TV, though. Soaps. Or shows where losers win. Or make-overs. Mom identifies with stuff like that. She wants to belong. I've actually never thought of it that way. I might be wrong.

It's cold out. My fingers feel frozen even with my hands stuffed in my pockets. There's bunches of leaves blowing around, scraping the sidewalk like fingernails on a chalkboard, which gives me major shivers. Even the streetlights make me think of ice.

I hear their guitars a few houses away from Cory's. They don't sound bad. But right now I feel like turning around and going back home.

I get to Cory's driveway and see the side door of

the garage open, so I walk in before I can change my mind. The sound goes suddenly from blasting guitars to nothing.

"Told you she'd come," says Leo.

Cory sets up a microphone. He's got an electric guitar and Leo's got a regular one. There's an amplifier and extension cords and a lawn mower and a snow blower and a workbench that looks identical to Dad's, all piled with tools and cans of paint, so there's really no space left to work on.

"If I'm just lip-syncing, what's this mic for?"

"We need a singer," says Leo.

"I'm not a singer."

"You don't have to be a singer, you just have to sing," says Cory, handing me the lyrics. "You come in after this riff." He plays something unrecognizable but excellent. "It's in A major. Try it." He gives me the chord.

I do nothing. What am I doing here?

"Come on, Emily. It's easy." He gives me the chord again.

When I do nothing again, he starts back at the riff and this time Leo plays along with him.

I stand in front of the microphone, facing the big garage doors, and make myself try the first line. Disaster.

"Too low," says Leo. "Let's try it in C." He gives me the C chord and hums it.

I'm remembering how much I used to like singing in elementary school with Miss Taylor giving us the note on her little harmonica. I try again.

"Close," says Cory.

"Let's just listen to the song all the way through," says Leo.

Cory pushes in the CD and unplugs his guitar from the amplifier. He plays silently except for the soft, squealing sound of his fingers on the strings of his electric guitar.

"Okay, let's try again," says Leo. "Ready?"

"Not really," I say. But no one's listening.

"One, two. One, two, three."

Their guitars start, one like an echo of the other. And then they're together. Precision. High notes like wind howling through telephone wires. Gusts and blasts of wind. Then quieter and Leo's large fingers move up the neck of his guitar and slide down. Cory brings in a few howls through the telephone wires. I hear the riff and get ready.

My voice through the microphone is like it isn't mine. It's bigger. And smoother. Then it wobbles and falls flat.

The guitars stop, with a note or two still floating up out of the amplifier before it's totally quiet.

"Don't think about your voice." Leo's obviously

SYLVIA GUNNERY

read my mind. "Just think about what the song means."

"And breathe," says Cory.

"But don't suck in air in front of the mic."

"One, two. One, two, three."

By the eleventh or thirteenth try, I'm making it all the way through the song, mostly because Cory and Leo don't stop when I mess up. When the song works and my voice is with the guitars, I can really feel it. I sing at those garage doors like there's an audience there. Thousands of people.

Cory and Leo have this kind of wave going as we come into the last two lines. This feels amazing. Cory does the ending riff and I add in the last word of the last line again, only softer. Leo gives us a couple of tumbling notes and then a single final note.

"Yes!"

I face the garage doors and shout into the mic, "Thank you! Thank you! On guitars behind me—Cory Bell and Leo Mac. I'm Emily Sinclair. Thank you! Good night!"

We're all grinning.

"That rocked, man," says Leo.

And I haven't even thought about Brian ... except for right this second.

* * *

Leo and I walk to the end of Cory's driveway and turn in the same direction, which is heading to where I live. I don't know where Leo lives. He's carrying his guitar in a canvas case that hangs off his shoulder. I don't really know what to say to him at first, so I go for the obvious. "Why'd you transfer to our school?"

"Had to."

"How come?"

"They say I have anger issues," says Leo flatly. "Some light bulb thinks changing schools'll change me. Stupid idiot."

I'm not sure how to respond to that. I can't figure Leo out. Being next to him right now is like being next to a bear. A tame bear. He's so tall and big. But maybe he could forget the fact that he's tame.

Out of nowhere he says, "You need to know you're not my type."

"What're you talking about?"

"Just what I said."

"I know what you said, but I don't have a clue why you said it." My cheeks are burning red. Who does this guy think he is? "You don't think I've got the hots for you, do you?"

"Not yet."

"Oh, like you can see it coming and this is some kind of warning for me. Well, you're so wrong!"

SYLVIA GUNNERY

"Okay then, I'm wrong."

We keep walking without saying anything. I'm trying not to be mad, but this is a very touchy subject for me right now. Very. I can't help it. And no way am I explaining anything to Leo about me and Brian.

I picture Brian this very minute, walking down a street in Montreal with his French girlfriend. Maybe his arm is around her and she's very small and fits right up against him like a jigsaw puzzle.

I feel like I'm walking in deep water and a wave of sadness is crashing over me.

"My street's down this way," I say.

"Right. When's English tomorrow?"

"Second class."

"Okay. See ya."

Leo crosses the street with his hands in his pockets and his shoulders hunched up and the guitar hanging on his back. Watching him gives me this lonely feeling.

When I get home, Dad's standing in the kitchen eating toast and drinking milk, meaning he's pretty sure he'll have a hard time getting to sleep. The TV in the living room's off so Mom's already in bed.

"Hungry?" Dad asks.

"Not really," I say.

"How'd your school project go?"

"Okay."

34

His face is all saggy and he's holding the piece of toast like it weighs a ton. Usually he has green eyes, pale green like mine, but right now they're gray. I know what he's thinking about, but I don't know what to say.

He takes a drink of milk. "I can see how confused and hurt our mother would've been if she saw Dad with another woman. She probably wanted to get out of there and just drive. Shake off those awful feelings before she had to face us kids."

"It makes sense," I say. *With another woman.* No one's said exactly what was going on when my grandmother looked in that window but it isn't impossible to figure out.

Dad just looks at me with his pale gray eyes and his saggy face.

What I'm wearing is so lame. This short black skirt and black boots and a tight white top and this wispy turquoise scarf tied around my waist. My hair is falling across my eye and you can only see one of my earrings dangling down. I look like a rock-star wannabe. Delusional.

And this morning I had to take the bus because Jenn has a dentist appointment.

Cory's waiting outside English class with his guitar

and the other gear for our project. "Hey, you look awesome!" He's delusional. "You see Leo yet?"

When English class starts, Leo's still not here. When it's our turn to do our project, he's still not here.

Cory doesn't even take his guitar out of its case. "We'll just play this CD. Forget the live music," he says. "I'll just say stuff about the song and then you do the bit about how it fits the play. We'll fake it from there."

"Sure."

"Don't say anything to Mr. Canning about practice or about Leo. I hate it when people suck up and make excuses," says Cory.

We do okay. Our project's boring but accurate.

"How'd the English project go? You look hot," says Jenn. Everyone's delusional today.

"Leo didn't show so we just did the basic blah, blah, blah. No live music." I take off the turquoise scarf and cram it into my backpack.

"Let's go somewhere and get lunch," she says.

I pick up this very miniscule sound in her voice and I know she's got something to tell me that she thinks I won't like. "What's up?"

She's walking away.

"Something going on?"

"Wait," she says.

When we're in her car, she doesn't start it. She looks

straight ahead like we're out there in traffic. "Okay," she says, "I had sex with Ronny last night."

It's obvious she thinks this is shocking news (okay, it is shocking) and that it's going to break my heart (give me a break).

"That's hysterical," I say, but I'm not laughing.

"Are you mad?"

"Why should I be mad?"

"I don't know. Maybe because of last Friday."

"I already told you nothing happened. Besides, I'm not interested in Ronny."

"He's sexy," she says a bit defensively.

"When he's sober," I say a bit aggressively.

"Look, if you're going to—"

"No. No. I'm sorry."

We're quiet for a minute.

"I'm not really hungry," she says.

"Me either."

I see Leo coming down the hall before Cory does. Almost everyone's already in class except for a few people grabbing things from their lockers.

"Oh yeah, so now you show up," says Cory. "Thanks a lot, loser."

Leo gives him this wild glare.

"Take it easy, you guys," I say. "The project's over. Forget it."

"I could've flunked because of you," says Cory.

"Oh, yeah? So am I the reason you flunked last year too?"

Cory's caught by this. Surprised. He slams his hand against Leo's chest. Leo pushes it away. This is no fair match. If Leo explodes, there'll be debris everywhere.

Cory dives into Leo and they fall hard against the wall.

Mrs. Delva comes out of her classroom shouting, "Boys! Boys! What's going on here? Cory, let go. Listen to me."

Some people are squashed at the doorway of Mrs. Delva's classroom, trying to see this whole scene.

Cory lets go and takes a step back. His face is blotched red and he's not looking at Leo. Leo is watching Cory's every move.

Mrs. Delva turns to the spectators in her doorway. "Go back to your seats, please. All of you." She closes the door. "Cory, I want you to walk in that direction. Cool yourself down. When this class is over, I expect to see you in Ms. Crosby's office and we'll hear your explanation for this attack. Emily and Leo, please walk in the other direction. No doubt Ms. Crosby will want to hear from both of you as well."

No one moves for a second, then we all follow her orders like she's a traffic cop. I'm wishing she'd asked me to walk with Cory instead of Leo.

We're just about at the end of the hall when Leo says, "That guy's a friggin' hothead."

"Oh, right. Like he got mad about nothing." Because it was my project too. Then, before I can stop myself, I say, "At least he doesn't have anger issues."

Leo takes off ahead of me. I'm already late for French class, but before I go down the stairs I make sure there's a lot of space between him and me.

In last class, Ms. Crosby comes on the PA and says she wants to see me. Embarrassing.

Leo's outside her office but I don't look at him. I sit as far away as I can.

She asks him to go in first.

While I'm waiting, I think about the fight, playing everything in my mind because she'll be asking me how it started. Well, Leo didn't show up for our project. But Cory called him a loser. Then Leo goes and makes that remark about Cory flunking last year. In a way, both of them started the fight.

Leo comes out of the office and walks away.

I tell Ms. Crosby the details I remember. Then she says, "Did you and Cory take the time to ask Leo why he wasn't in school for the English project?" Which means that whatever kept him from showing up this morning is no lame excuse. And it's something she's not going to tell us if Leo doesn't.

On my way back to class, I think about last night, how Leo was walking across the street alone, carrying his guitar, all hunched up against the cold. I get this sad feeling because he's probably alone like that a lot and there must be more stuff than just a cold night he has to protect himself from.

Today in English class, Leo sat by himself near the window and Mr. Canning didn't make him move back to the table with Cory and me. News travels. Cory was obviously still ticked off but he didn't talk about it. The more I looked at Leo over there by himself, the worse I felt about saying what I said to him about anger issues. I don't want the guy to hate me.

Jenn had to go to work after fourth class so I'm taking the bus home. Leo's at the bus stop. He's ignoring me. Surprise.

"Look, I shouldn't've said what I said yesterday. After the fight."

"I didn't start that fight."

"You didn't show up for our project."

"I didn't start the fight."

"So how come you weren't in English class?"

"Complications." He looks in the direction that the bus will be coming. "May as well walk," he says to himself and turns around and leaves.

The bus comes and I get on. Leo ignores the roar of the bus as it passes by because he knows if he looks up he'll see me sitting here looking out at him.

Four

Halloween used to be better than Christmas. You got to dress up and go out in the dark where everything felt so strange. Shadows and streetlights. Kids in costumes knocking on doors. Trick or treat!

I'm the one in charge of giving out candy. Dad was never into this, and now Mom has me as an excuse not to answer the door and pretend to be amazed and say, "What do we have here? Oh, my, a monster!" when all the time you know it's Sam or Finn from down the street.

Two kids dressed up as teddy bears are holding their pillowcases open. I say, "I don't think teddy bears eat candy. I'm sure they only eat berries."

One of the kids pulls off her mask and says, "I'm not a teddy bear. I'm Lily." That cracks me up.

I grab another handful of candy, and then I see

Leo walking along beside a small pink rabbit. The rabbit's got long, floppy ears and sparkly whiskers and it's holding a basket. They turn and walk toward our door, where I'm standing with this handful of candy kisses and a surprised look on my face.

For a second there's an awkward silence. Leo's obviously surprised to see me too.

"Hi, pink rabbit," I say. "Sorry I don't have any carrots tonight. Just boring ol' candy kisses. I don't think rabbits eat candy kisses." Why not go for the same trick twice?

The pink rabbit looks up at Leo with a worried frown. I'm thinking she might cry.

Leo says, "Tell her you're a candy-eating rabbit and that carrots suck."

All she does is look into her almost-empty basket. I dump a huge handful of candy kisses in there, and the rabbit looks at me and smiles. Her nose is painted pink on the very tip. She's so cute.

"Say thank you," says Leo.

"Thank you," says the rabbit.

"You're welcome, little pink candy-eating rabbit," I say.

Another bunch of trick-or-treaters are crowding up on our doorstep as Leo and the rabbit walk away. There's a pirate, a gypsy, and a sailor who looks too old to be out trick-or-treating. I dump stuff into their bags, thinking that the rabbit must be Leo's sister. It's funny thinking of Leo with a pink-rabbit sister.

In English class, Cory and I still sit at the same table and Leo still sits alone over by the window. I don't say much to Cory these days. Not that we were ever best buds, anyway.

When the bell rings, I time it so I'm at the door just when Leo gets there. He isn't fooled.

"Who was that rabbit you were with last night?" I try to make this sound like a corny joke.

"Caroline."

"She your sister?"

"Yeah."

"She's cute."

"Yeah."

What am I doing? He obviously doesn't want to talk to me.

Leo keeps on walking and I'm still beside him for about three more steps. Then I fake forgetting something and say, "Oh, darn. I forgot something in English," and I go back all the way into the classroom and stand there like an idiot.

Mr. Canning is erasing the board and looks at me

over his elbow. "Do you need something, Emily?"

"Ah, no. I just thought I forgot something but I guess I didn't." I leave before I look even more ridiculous.

Leo's a couple of people ahead of me in the cafeteria line, giving me a sideways look. He thinks I'm stalking him. As if I need this.

"Look," I say when we're all the way through the line, "I'm trying to apologize for what I said the other day. I don't usually say sarcastic stuff like that."

He hesitates for a second. Then he says, "Let's go over here," and walks to an empty table.

I sit across from him, watching him jab a couple fries into a blob of ketchup. He's not looking at me.

I unwrap my tuna sandwich, lift the bread to make sure there's no extra mayonnaise, and take a small bite.

Leo smears another bunch of fries with ketchup.

I think of telling him that the ketchup they use in this cafeteria isn't the kind I like, and then I think of explaining how ketchup was invented in China a couple hundred years ago but it wasn't the same as the ketchup we have now.

By some miracle, I don't say anything.

"Caroline's almost six," says Leo. "She's small but she's smart." Now he's looking directly at me. "The reason I was late for English the other day is always the reason I'm late or don't show up."

I keep listening.

"What would you do if it was your sister and your mother's passed-out drunk on the sofa and it's seven in the morning?"

I picture the little pink bunny rabbit with a lipstick nose and floppy ears, looking down at her passed-out mother. It makes me feel extremely sad.

"And the friggin' counselors say I'm supposed to take anger management. Pisses me off!"

That makes me grin. I can't help it. Leo knows it's funny too, but he's trying not to smile.

I get rid of my grin and say, "They just want to help."

"How's anger management gonna help? Shit happens. You do anger management crap. The shit's still there. The anger's still there. Useless."

Right now Leo's eyes are dark wells. He's down in there somewhere and so's his little sister Caroline. It's like they'll be down in there forever unless their mom wakes up and sees them and holds out her hand.

Mom's putting icing on brownies when I walk in the kitchen, and I know it's her second batch because there's another pan on the counter and most of those brownies are gone. The reason they're gone isn't because friends suddenly dropped by to gab and eat brownies for an hour. She ate those brownies herself. It happens all the time. Her doctor tells her she wouldn't eat them if she didn't make them.

"Mmmm, brownies," I say, because I know she feels bad about eating so many and having to make more so there'd be some for me and Dad. I stick my finger into the bowl and lick the icing.

"Don't ruin your supper," she says, but she doesn't see the irony in this. She makes sure I learn all these good eating habits and read labels and avoid junk, while she does all the wrong things when it comes to food. Mom's always going on a diet but then going off it.

"I suppose Brian will be home as soon as his exams are finished. Have you two made any Christmas plans?"

This makes me just about die because I've been trying to blank Brian out of my mind. I already know that when he gets home I'll see him everywhere I go, and that's definitely not going to be fun. "It's too early to think about Christmas."

"You two got our tree last year. Maybe you'll—"

"We broke up."

"You what?"

"It wasn't working, Mom. He's there. I'm here."
She's there.

I don't go into details. Just talking about it gives me this sick feeling in my stomach because I'm the one who was dumped. If eating a whole pan of brownies would get rid of this sick feeling then I'd be stuffing my face right now.

"I see," says Mom, running water into the bowl and wiping off the icing spoon with a paper towel. Then she says, "You're young, Emily. You have plenty of time for other boyfriends in your life."

I try to get the conversation off the topic of Brian. "Did you have lots of boyfriends before you met Dad?"

"Not really." She's drying the bowl and I'm looking at how her wedding band is pinched on her finger.

Even though I just want to go to my room and squish down this sick feeling that's getting bigger and bigger in my stomach, I say, "Who did you like the most before Dad?"

"Oh, I don't remember."

"Come on, Mom. You gotta remember guys you liked."

"Well, maybe I didn't like any of them enough for that. One day when you don't remember Brian anymore, you'll know what I mean."

That wasn't fair, but I know she doesn't mean it like that. Facts are facts for Mom. No sense smoothing over a situation with sympathy or empathy or any other pathetic pity. Sometimes I wish I could be like that. You're cold, wear a sweater. You're warm, take the sweater off. You're dumped, get over it.

We're all sitting around the kitchen table, drinking tea and eating brownies. Dad and Aunt Em are figuring out what to do with Granddad's stuff from his apartment.

"I'll call Family Resources," says Aunt Em. "We could dry-clean clothes worth giving away. They also take furniture and distribute it. Is there anything of his you want?"

"I don't know," says Dad. "What about you?"

Mom cuts in and says, "Where would we have room for anything else in this house?"

We all know she doesn't want any reminders of Granddad around here.

"Didn't his will say where his stuff should go?" All of a sudden I realize I've opened a can of worms. More like a time bomb. There is definitely something weird about Granddad's will. I can see it on their faces. It takes about a half a second for me to guess. "Cynthia Maxwell's in Granddad's will, isn't she."

"Not exactly," says Dad.

"Cynthia Maxwell's daughter is named in Dad's will," says Aunt Em.

I suddenly connect the dots. "Ohmygawd."

"So," says Mom with a no-love-lost kind of voice, "your caring and thoughtful grandfather started his second family when your father and aunt were about fourteen. The quintessential family man."

Dad and Aunt Em look at Mom in a depressed, defeated sort of way. Who could blame them? First you find out your father had an affair for years and years, and then you find out you've got a sister you didn't know you had. Doesn't matter that it sounds like a corny cliché. It still hurts. I know what I'm talking about.

"Did Cynthia Maxwell have any other kids? I mean with her husband?"

"No."

"No wonder she was at Granddad's funeral. Why didn't the daughter come?"

Dad looks at Aunt Em and I can see another secret floating up.

"Don't tell me," I say. "Let me guess. She doesn't know that Granddad's her father. This is nuts."

"A soap opera," says Aunt Em, trying to squeeze out a smile.

"And Cynthia Maxwell doesn't want you guys to let this daughter know the illegitimate facts of her life." I'm on a roll. "She's bound to find out if she's in the will."

"Dad's lawyer is giving Mrs. Maxwell a bit of time

to deal with this," says Aunt Em.

Mom isn't saying anything now. She's just sipping her tea and not eating any brownies. Any more brownies.

I feel like we're sitting around this huge jigsaw puzzle with pieces scattered all over, and now this lost little piece has suddenly been snapped into place. Dad and Aunt Em's sister. Weird.

In the dream, I'm sound asleep here in bed. But I can still see because I'm watching Brian walking in through my bedroom door. He just comes and stands beside my bed. He's wearing his blue jacket and it's zipped up like it was cold when he was outside. I want to wake up and tell him how happy I am that he's back, how much I missed him. I want to hold him and feel him holding me. Only I can't move and I can't talk. It's like I'm trapped inside myself.

Even though I'm asleep, I realize that this is only a dream and that Brian isn't actually standing beside my bed. So I try to wake myself up. With all my might I try to shake my head, but it won't move. I keep trying and trying. It makes me panic. I shake my head and shake my head until suddenly I'm out of the dream. I'm here in my bed and of course Brian isn't here with me. He won't ever be with me. I can't stand it.

Then all of a sudden I feel like I have to get out of here. I haul on my clothes and quietly go downstairs. On purpose I don't have my cell with me. I put on my jacket and scarf and I go out. Sneak out.

Our neighborhood looks deserted. I don't see one single other person, which I figure is a good thing considering it's the middle of the night. The sound of my footsteps seems like it's coming from somewhere else. Disconnected. All along this part of the street is a tall, thick hedge, and the streetlight is making my shadow fall on it. It's like there's a person I don't know walking right beside me.

I remember when I was four or maybe five. Mom bought me new red rubber boots and a bright blue raincoat with a hat to match. I insisted on putting everything on that very afternoon and going out, even though it wasn't raining. I went down our front walk and turned and waved at Mom who was waving at me. She let me go the whole way around our block all alone. I wasn't afraid because I knew Mom was standing in our doorway, waiting for me to finally make it all the way back home.

I shiver because it's cold and because I'm afraid.

I'm not sure if this was such a good idea. I picture people in these houses waking up and peering out their windows and saying, *My goodness! That's Emily Sinclair*

out there, walking in the middle of the night all by herself.
Where is she going? Whatever is she thinking? Do her
parents know where she is?

This is possibly the weirdest thing I've ever done.

I start walking faster and faster until I've gone
all the way around the block and I can see our house
again.

When I get home, I very quietly go in and take off
my jacket and scarf. Then I tiptoe upstairs and get back
in bed.

I don't want to close my eyes. In case I dream about
Brian again.

When I go into the kitchen, Mom's sipping tea and
waiting for toast to pop up. I can tell she doesn't know
that I went out last night.

"Remember when you bought me that blue raincoat with the matching hat and the red rubber boots
and I walked around the block all by myself?"

"Of course I do. I called Mrs. Day over on Robie
Street to see if she could see you out her front door."

"I didn't know you did that."

She cuts a thin slice of cheese and places it on her
unbuttered toast. "Any mother would worry when her
child walks away out of sight for the very first time."

It feels sort of sad that Mom doesn't know I was out last night walking by myself. She would've been worried. And confused.

Even though it's sad and even though I'm potentially hurting her feelings, I know I'm not going to tell her.

Five

I haven't talked to Jenn for about a week and that's no coincidence. She drives Ronny to school now. I don't blame her. It's not like when we were in junior high and I'd go to movies with her and whichever guy had the hots for her that week. If I kept on doing that, I'd end up sitting in the backseat when she drives away on her honeymoon. Pathetic.

So I've been taking the bus to school. Most days Leo's there and I sit with him. We don't actually say much and I'm okay with that. When he's not there, like yesterday, I start wondering whether his mother is passed out and if he's getting Caroline ready for school. Guess there's no dad in the picture, but I'm not asking.

Today he's there at the back of the bus when I get on. I say, "Geez, I'm glad it's Friday."

He says, "Yeah."

"You doing anything this weekend?" As soon as the words are out of my mouth, I realize that he could take it the wrong way. "I'm just asking. Not like I'm—"

"I'm hitching to my aunt's place tomorrow. Caroline's living there now. They came to get her yesterday." Every word is loaded with some kind of anger mixed with desperation.

When I try to picture Caroline, she's still in that rabbit costume. I see her with a little suitcase packed and she's bawling and crying because she doesn't want to leave Leo. I know I'm right about the crying part because it was as plain as anything that she worships her big brother. And he adores her.

Life's for sure not simple.

After last class, Leo comes up behind me when I'm putting stuff in my locker.

"Wanna come to my aunt's tomorrow?"

"What?"

"I didn't think you would." He starts to walk away.

"Wait! What're you talking about?"

"Thought you might be bored all by yourself. It's not like you and Barbie'd have plans."

"Barbie?"

"Your old best friend. Barbie...and Ken."

I half-laugh at this. Which tells me I'm not much of a friend if I'm so ready to laugh at Jenn. Then I realize

I'm actually thinking of going to Leo's aunt's with him. Why not? "Where does your aunt live?"

"Past Hubbards."

I don't tell Leo that I've never hitchhiked before.

It's still early and pretty cold when we get out on the highway. It's really strange walking on the side of the road like this. I feel like we're stranded. Cars whiz past like we're not even here.

My hands are freezing. I pull my collar up against my ears and hunch my shoulders. Hubbards is about an hour from here if we're lucky enough to get one ride that takes us all the way. For a second, I think of calling Dad and asking him to come get me. But I decide not to, mostly because Leo'd think I'm a wimp.

Leo gets me to stand in front of him. He says that's so he won't look like a criminal. I'm hoping whoever picks us up doesn't look like a criminal.

A car stops with a woman driver and a dog in the passenger seat. The dog's a Rottweiler.

"Don't worry. Nella's harmless unless I tell her not to be."

Leo makes me get in first. The dog turns around and stares like she's figuring out who I am and if I have any weird plans. She has these cute little brownish spots above those dark scary eyes.

When Leo gets in, the dog makes a little rumble growl.

"That's fine, Nella," says the woman. "Lie down. There you go."

The dog obeys.

"Where are you going?"

"Exit six," says Leo.

"I can take you to exit four."

We're stuck at exit four for almost half an hour.

Then a van stops, with a guy driving and a little boy in the front seat. Leo slides the door open and we climb in. The little boy checks us out. The guy waits until we have our seatbelts on, then pulls out behind a truck.

"Where you goin'?"

"Exit six," says Leo.

"Zak and me are goin' right past there."

Perfect. The heater's blasting and already my fingers are thawing from being cramped-up claws in my pockets. Leo's sitting back, looking out the window. There's nothing to see out there but trees, trees, and more trees.

"You live in Hubbards?" the guy asks.

"No," says Leo.

That microscopically short answer sounds a bit rude when you think this person just stopped and picked us up and saved us from freezing out there for who knows how long. So I get a bit chatty and say, "We're going to see Leo's little sister who's at his aunt's."

Leo glares at me so I won't talk about something that's not my business, and I get his point.

"We're visiting too, hey, Zak," the guy says with a sideways glance at the boy, probably to check how he's doing now with two strangers in the van. Zak doesn't say anything. He's only about seven. Maybe eight.

The guy keeps on talking. "We're going to see Mommy. We'll all go to our favorite restaurant and have pizza with the works, hey, Zak."

Zak says, "Mm."

And right now I know for a fact that Leo's thinking about Caroline and wondering about when she'll get to visit her mom.

The guy turns up the radio, which is a relief because now we can just sit back here and not talk. Leo's favorite thing to do.

I suddenly feel weird in this van with a bunch of people I don't actually know, going somewhere I don't know to see more people I don't know. I stare out the window and think about what Mom and Dad would do if they knew where I was right now. If they met Leo, maybe they'd be okay with it. Especially if I told them about how he takes care of his little sister.

I glance over at Leo and give him a kind of half-smile. He gives me a what's-with-you look. But I don't try to explain.

When the guy lets us out at exit six, I wave to Zak as they drive away, but he just looks at me like I'm cardboard. Then Leo tells me we have to walk down the ramp and start hitchhiking on the old highway.

"Where's your aunt's house, exactly?"

"North West Cove."

"You said Hubbards."

"Near Hubbards, I said."

It turns out that North West Cove is only near Hubbards if you're getting there by helicopter. And it also turns out that not many people drive on this old highway. Before we get a ride, my body has lots of time to practically freeze.

Leo pushes on the doorbell over and over and over as he walks in. We're standing on a small landing with stairs going down into a dark basement and three steps up into a kitchen. There are boots and shoes and sneakers—a very small pink pair—left on the landing. Leo hauls off his boots so I take off my shoes.

We hear her voice, "Leo! Leo! Leo! Leo! Leo! Leo!" and then we see her. Caroline jumps into his arms before he has a chance to get all the way into the kitchen. She has dark hair with thick curls and two rainbow barrettes holding some of those curls back. Even though she's very little, she looks a lot like Leo. Same eyes. Same mouth.

Then she notices me and gets this serious look on her face.

"That's Emily. She's the one who tried to cop out on giving you candies on Halloween."

"I was only joking," I say a bit defensively. Don't little kids get jokes like that?

"Look what the wind blew in."

Leo puts Caroline down and turns to me. "This is Emily. Emily, this is Jane."

"Hi," I say.

"Nice to meet you," she says.

I can tell she's not trying to figure out who I am. I'm there. I'm with Leo for whatever reason. That's it. If this was Mom, there'd be question marks all over her face.

"I don't like when you hitchhike, Leo."

"How else'm I supposed to get here? Besides, Emily was there to guarantee a ride." He smirks at me like he just got away with something. One hand is still on Caroline's head and she's swivelling around like a dancer under his palm.

All his aunt does is sigh. "Take off your jackets. I'll make scrambled eggs and hot chocolate. Caroline, go turn off the TV and show Leo your spelling test."

"You had a test already? Did you flunk?" says Leo.

"Silly," says Caroline, and leads him by the hand out of the kitchen.

"I can help," I say.

"Sure." She takes eggs out of the fridge and puts a frying pan on the stove.

"Leo just started at my school a couple weeks ago. We're friends, not like girlfriend and boyfriend."

"That I figured out."

"Really?"

She smiles and says, "But I can see he likes you, so I like you too."

I'm a bit disgusted with myself about feeling all warm and fuzzy because she thinks Leo likes me. There's nothing wrong with being liked. I like Leo too.

We stay for a couple hours and I entertain myself by guessing things about Leo's aunt. She's not married. No ring. She has a man in her life because on a shelf there's a picture with her and him hugging on a beach with winter coats on. She doesn't smoke. No ashtrays.

Caroline isn't asking anything about her mother, and Leo and his aunt aren't saying anything about her, either. Then, when Caroline's in the bathroom out of hearing distance, Leo's aunt says, "Your father wants Caroline to go live with him."

"Crap!"

"Shhh," she says. "Caroline…"

"That fuckin' idiot!"

"Leo, watch your mouth!" She says this in the loudest whisper she can manage.

"It's stupid. How's it gonna help anything? He's on the road all the time."

"When he's away, she'll stay here."

"Oh, great. Just great. Ping-Pong anyone?"

Caroline's still in the bathroom, and I'm thinking she's taking an extra-long time. Leo's aunt's thinking the same thing because she gets up and walks down the hall.

"The guy's a fuckin' idiot." Leo says this to me like it explains everything.

Caroline comes back up the hall with Jane and it's obvious she heard the main points of the conversation. She's looking at Leo like he's already further away.

"Come here," he says and hauls her up on his knee, even though she's almost too big for that. She leans her head against his chest. "Right now we'll do whatever Jane says, okay? She's got a good head on her shoulders. Not like her dumb-ass brother. And not like your dumb-ass brother, either."

Caroline lifts her head and smiles into Leo's face.

This just about breaks my heart.

When we go to leave, Jane tells us to wait so Dan can drive us back to the city. But Leo says that there's lots of time to hitchhike back before dark.

I'm figuring Dan's the guy in the picture.

"At least let me call Angela. She'll drive you out to the 103."

Maybe it's the relieved look on my face that makes him give in. "Tell her we'll meet her by the government wharf," he says. "Save her coming over here."

Caroline's all quiet as we leave. Leo's telling her he'll phone at the usual time and he'll see her in a few days. No one's mentioned the father again.

We get to the wharf and it's pretty windy. Whoever Angela is, she's not here yet. Lobster traps are stacked high in neat, tight rows beside where boats are tied up. *Rose Krista. Double B. Homeward Bound.* High waves are pounding against the breakwater that's protecting this little cove.

"That's you out there, Leo," I say.

"What're you talking about?"

"When you get mad. All those waves crashing in, over and over and over, exploding on those rocks."

For a second he doesn't say anything. Then he picks up a small rock and puts it roughly in my hand. "That's what getting mad feels like. Not waves crashing or exploding. It's a rock right here in your guts."

A car horn toots behind us. Leo walks over and gets in the front. The driver, who must be Angela, throws a cigarette butt out her window. I get in the backseat, still holding the rock in my fist.

"This is Emily," says Leo. "This is Angela."

"Hi," I say. "Thanks for the drive."

"Sorry I can't take you all the way into the city."

"We won't have a problem once we're on the 103," says Leo.

This time he doesn't joke about me guaranteeing a lift. I know he's still fuming about what I said. Which sort of proves I'm right.

I open my hand and take a closer look at the rock. It's mostly white, with little gray and black flecks all over it. Some of them catch the light and sparkle. It's beautiful. I put it in my jacket pocket and look out at the gray ocean and the gray sky and the gray shoreline going past.

Dad's in the backyard filling his bird feeders when I get home. He does this twice a day. "Breakfast and supper," he says. I like how birds know the routine. It even seems like they know him.

"You're home," says Dad.

"Yeah."

"Pretty good day?"

"Not bad," I say. "I went with a friend of mine, Leo, to see his little sister. She's living at his aunt's now because his mom's an alcoholic." I don't say anything about hitchhiking. "His sister might have to go live with her father who Leo says is an idiot."

"Sounds complicated," says Dad. He pours some black sunflower seeds from his hand into mine.

"It made me feel sad." I stretch out my arm and hold up my handful of seeds.

"It is sad," he says.

There's a whir of little wings as a chickadee lands on the tips of my fingers. It grabs a seed and whirs away. I watch it land on a branch and pound the shell to get at the food inside. Then another chickadee lands. Its thin black legs and feet make me think of pencil doodles on a page.

Dad's just standing there, watching the chickadees land on my fingers and take off, land and take off.

"I don't remember you saying anything about some-one called Leo," says Dad.

"He's new at school. We're friend-friends," I say to make things clear. I toss the rest of the seeds on the grass and put my cold hands into my pockets. Leo's an-ger rock is still there.

"I see."

"He can be very funny when he wants to, but a lot of the time he sort of stews."

"Makes sense with all that's going on with his family."

"His little sister adores him."

"That'll probably get him through the complications."

"Yeah," I say.

"Your mom told me about you and Brian, Emily. I always liked Brian. But whatever reason he has for changing his mind, it's got nothing to do with you...who you are, what you look like, nothing. Who knows what people want? Sometimes even they don't know themselves." He picks up the bag of seeds and starts toward the house.

I know Dad said all this to make me feel better. And I want to feel better. But now he's got me thinking about how people want stuff. How I want Brian.

But, if he was here, his new girlfriend would be right beside him, holding his hand and saying, *Pardonez-moi*. I feel stupid when I think that what I want in my whole life is just this one certain person. It's making me nuts.

When I wake up in the middle of the night, I get it in my head that I want to go out for a walk again, even though it's cold and dark and deserted out there.

I'm very quiet as I leave the house.

This time I don't stay on our block. I cross at the flashing red lights and walk past our elementary school, down over the hill, and along one of the boulevards with skeleton trees and dark houses.

At the end of the boulevard, I turn up the street

69

where it's not as deserted and quiet because it's a main route from the bridge to downtown. A bus goes by with nobody in it except the driver.

I'm getting cold now. Leo's anger rock is in my hand that's stuffed into my pocket because I didn't, as usual, wear mittens or gloves.

I hear a car slowing down before I notice headlights sliding along the curb beside me. My heart jumps into my throat. I keep walking.

"Hey. Hey. Need a drive?" The voice sounds like a guy maybe my age. "Hey!" He says it louder this time.

The car is right beside me now but I don't look.

"We're just asking if you need a drive. We won't hurt you."

This just makes things worse because now I know there's more than one person in the car.

A couple other cars go by but no one seems to notice how I'm being harassed by whoever's in this car. I hold Leo's anger rock tightly in my hand. If these guys try anything, at least I have this rock.

I see a house with a wide glassed-in porch and decide to pretend I live there. I go up the steps, put my hand on the doorknob, and turn it. By some miracle, the door opens and I step inside. There are old wicker chairs, empty planters, a snow shovel, and a rake leaning in a corner. The porch isn't heated. Over my shoulder I can see the car moving slowly away.

My heart's pounding. I sit in one of the chairs and try to calm down. There's no sound in the house. Maybe no one's home.

After a while, I look out the window, up and down the street. Maybe the car's waiting somewhere close by. Maybe they know I'm faking living here. I'm wishing I had my cell with me. But then I think I probably wouldn't call Mom and Dad in the middle of the night, anyway, and scare them half to death when they think I'm right down the hall, sleeping in my bed.

Very quietly and slowly, I go outside. I head back the way I came, speeding up a bit when I get to the boulevard and start up the hill. My heart's still pounding as I cross at the flashing red lights and head toward my street.

When I close the front door behind me and gently turn the lock, I'm shivering from the inside out.

Six

Aunt Em arranged for all of us to have lunch at Harmony Hills with Meredith to celebrate her birthday. She's always doing family stuff like this. Once I asked her why she's not living with someone or why she didn't get married, and she said that life gave her a dessert bowl but not a dinner plate. I think she's just content with what she's got: her cat, her job, a couple of friends, and us.

Mom made carrot cake with orange-flavored icing between the two layers and on top. In pink icing it says *Happy Birthday Meredith* with *88* written under that. Toothpicks are keeping the waxed paper up off the icing. If I hold the cake plate in my hands and don't set it down on my lap, I can prevent it from sliding when Dad makes a turn, or falling totally on the floor if he has to come to a sudden stop. Suspension. Dad showed me this trick when we were taking a cake to Aunt Em's for one of their birthdays a hundred years ago.

The dining room at Harmony Hills is pleasant. That's Mom's word. Aunt Em refers to it as cheerful. Dad says it gets the job done.

There's a table for the five of us with balloons tied to our chairs and with birthday napkins—all arranged by Aunt Em sometime this morning. Meredith is at the head of the table with Dad on one side of her and Aunt Em on the other. I'm beside Dad and Mom's across from me.

Meredith picks up her napkin and inspects the pattern.

"Those are your birthday napkins," says Aunt Em cheerfully. "And your balloon says *Happy Birthday* too." She pulls on the ribbon until the balloon is in front of Meredith.

She smiles at the balloon and then at all of us. "Lovely," she says.

I notice a table near ours where three ladies are sitting together, each wearing a large, colorful bib. One of them has just said, "My husband died in my arms and I'll never forgive him."

I'm trying to figure out which one of them said that.

Women in hairnets deliver bowls of corn chowder with a roll and tea or coffee. Aunt Em gets up and ties a green bib on Meredith. Meredith smoothes it down and then looks at her fingernails, which Aunt Em painted bright pink before we all came down to this dining room. Except for not knowing everything that's going on, Meredith is a very gracious lady. She hasn't forgotten about table manners and which spoon is for chowder and which one is for tea. She eats slowly, sipping small spoonfuls.

"How do you like your chowder, Meredith?" asks Aunt Em. "Delicious, isn't it?"

"Not as good as what you used to make, though," Dad says. "Onions. That's the secret ingredient. You fried your onions first. I remember that."

"Onions wouldn't agree with most of these elderly people," says Mom.

"I suppose," says Dad. "Here, let me do that." He gently takes the butter from Meredith and pulls the foil off the top. Then he holds the container while she puts some butter on her knife and spreads it across the roll she has divided in two.

I'm mesmerized right now by the fact that the butter is served in those little plastic thingies that probably half the people here can't peel the tops off of. Milk and cream for tea and coffee are in the same type of containers. And sugar is in little packets that have to be ripped open. Is anybody paying attention here?

"My husband died in my arms and I'll never forgive him."

This time I saw which person was speaking. She's looking at the lady beside her and that lady just shrugged one of her shoulders. It wasn't like shrugging two shoulders which would've meant, *Who knows?* That one-shoulder shrug was like saying, *That's the way it goes.*

Corn chowder isn't high on my list of things to eat, but this bowl is small so I manage to finish most of it.

"If you don't want your roll, I'll have it," Dad says to me. "No sense wasting it."

He added that bit about wasting food because he knows Mom would be ready to say something about watching his carbs. Which would be a bit pointless, considering that this lunch consists of corn chowder, rolls, and carrot cake. Carb city.

"How old am I?" Meredith is watching Aunt Em light the candles. There are six of them for some illogical reason.

"Eighty-eight!" says Aunt Em enthusiastically because Meredith has just said something that makes sense.

"Oops," says Meredith with a grin and a twinkle, as if getting to be eighty-eight was some kind of accident. "How old is your father?"

Everyone around the table looks at everyone else.

Dad takes the challenge and says, "Dad'd be eighty-six on his next birthday."

"Imagine," says Meredith. "Where is he? Is he at work?"

"No. He's not at work," says Dad slowly. "He…"

The six candles are flickering and beginning to drip on the icing.

Aunt Em starts singing "Happy Birthday to You" and we join in. The whole dining room sings along, with people turning around to look at our table, where Aunt Em is holding the cake with flickering candles, and five balloons are floating above our heads. Dad and Aunt Em blow out the candles, and everyone gives Meredith a big round of applause.

"…my arms and I'll never forgive him," I hear as the clapping fades.

When we're driving away from Harmony Hills, Aunt Em says, "Oh, my," inside this huge sigh.

"She's doing all right," says Dad reassuringly.

"It's not that. I know she's fine. It's just…"

"Memories are the problem," says Mom. "You have to put those aside and only think of now. She is not the same person she used to be—none of us is, for that matter. But she's contented and comfortable. That's all we need to think of."

"Easier said than done," says Aunt Em.

I have to agree with Aunt Em on this one. It's the same with Brian. I can go along for a while, like the past couple of hours, and I don't think about him. But then all of a sudden I remember something, his hair or his eyes or something he did or said, and my throat gets all tight and I have to take a deep breath. It's impossible to only think of now.

"That's a lot of memories to put aside," says Dad quietly. "Meredith's been part of our lives a long, long time. Hope when I'm in a nursing home and I've lost most of my marbles, someone'll come have lunch with me and then heave a big sigh afterwards, remembering some of the good times."

I reach forward and scratch the back of Dad's head and say, "I'll come, Dad. And I'll remember stuff." But I can't even picture Dad in a nursing home. Wearing a bib? No way.

We get all quiet in the car.

"I'm just saying it's a way to cope with the situation," says Mom. "It's up to yourselves what you do."

"Emily," says Dad very seriously. "I have a request."

"What?"

"When I'm in the nursing home, I want you to remember the time your mom decided to touch up the paint on those yellow lawn chairs and then didn't put the top back on the can of paint tight enough."

"And you shook it to mix the paint up and it spilled and splashed all over the place. Well, mostly all over you. Your hair, your face — "

"You stank of paint remover for days!" says Aunt Em, laughing.

"That's the last paint job your mom ever did."

"I was ever allowed to do," says Mom.

"Oh, look," I say. "It's snowing."

Small flakes are falling gently down. I love the first snowfall. It always makes me feel quiet and calm and sort of excited all at once. Like something magical's happening even though snow falling down is the most ordinary thing.

"Old man winter," says Dad.

I sit back and look out at the snow, trying to make this feeling last.

When I woke up last night, I got out of bed and looked out my window at the quiet, white street. It had stopped snowing and there wasn't much on the ground, but it was enough that there were tracks where a car had stopped at the corner and turned. Part of me wanted to go out and leave my boot tracks all along the deserted sidewalk. But I crawled back into bed and went to sleep again.

This morning Leo's on the bus with his guitar in that black case on the seat beside him. I can take a hint. He's looking out the window as if there's something important happening out there. I can take two hints.

I sit a few seats in front of him and slouch down. I'm tired. Not exhausted, but tired of stuff that's going on. I'm tired of Brian and his Montreal girlfriend and the fact that he'll be back home for Christmas in a few weeks and I'll have to deal with that. I'm tired of going to school and listening to people talking about applying to universities or keeping marks up for scholarships or living in dorms next year or finding apartments. I'm tired of Leo back there on this bus, sitting beside his guitar so there's no room for me because he's mad about what I said about how his anger's going to explode.

The anger rock is still here in my pocket. I like how it feels in my hand. Even though I can't see the little sparkly bits, I know they're there. No way I would've thrown this rock at whoever those loser guys were the other night. Not unless I was sure I could go back and find it again.

When the bus stops I go out the front door, because I know Leo will be going out the back. I'm curious about why he brought his guitar to school, but I'm not asking him about it. Or anything else.

* * *

Jenn's at her locker and Ronny's nowhere in sight. "Hey!" she says with a big grin. "Emily! Hi!"

"What's with the cheerleading?" I say.

"Cheerleading?"

"Never mind. Where's Ronny?"

"Flu."

"Flew where?"

"Very funny," she says with an even wider grin. "I said flu. As in cold and flu. He's staying home. So what's new with you? I've seen you hanging around with that Leo guy."

"He's not my boyfriend."

"I didn't say he was. I'm just saying I saw you."

"It's the way you said it."

"What way?"

"You know what I mean. Stop playing brain-dead."

"You're in some awful mood."

"Yeah." By now I've taken what I need from my locker and all I want to do is get to class. It's English, speaking of Leo. Fun and games. "Well, gotta go. See ya."

"Wait a minute, Emily. Just because we haven't been hanging out doesn't mean we're not friends anymore."

"But that's what friends do, Jenn. They hang out. At least once in a while." Now I sound like a simpering kid when really it doesn't matter to me that I'm not hanging out with Jenn. I've got too much on my mind. "I didn't mean that the way it sounded," I say. "I've just got a lot on my mind."

"Meaning Brian?"

"Not just him."

"Look, how about we go somewhere at lunch. Grab something to eat."

"I brought a salad."

"Come on, Emily."

The bell for first class cuts off our conversation, so I just say, "Okay."

"Great," she says. "Meet you here at twelve."

I get to English class and stop dead in my tracks. Leo's sitting by himself at his usual table over by the window, but he's strumming his guitar. What's up with this?

Mr. Canning's checking off names in his register as everyone comes into the room. The late bell goes and he closes the classroom door. Then he announces that he has given Leo permission to present the *Romeo and Juliet* project he missed. "Leo tells me he has written a piece of music for solo guitar to reflect the soundscape of Shakespeare's play," he says.

Cory is slouched down in his chair. His eyes are closed and his arms are folded across his chest. If he was allowed to wear his hat in class, it'd be pulled down over his face right now.

But I'm curious about what Leo's about to do. I didn't know he could write music.

He picks up the round stool that Mr. Canning usually sits on when he's talking at us and places it at the front of the class. He sits on the edge of the stool and tucks the heel of his boot onto a rung. Then he strums a couple of times and twists a knob or two on the neck of the guitar.

"*Romeo and Juliet* is a play that's like a river," he says, looking down at his guitar. Then he looks up at us and says, "Sometimes it flows along, no problem, and other times it hits rocks and boulders and cra—stuff like that, and things get rough. There's emotions too. Rivalry. Love. First falling in love and then being in love. Then anger and fear and confusion and despair. For this project I translated all that into musical notes. So here it is."

I'm listening and I'm amazed. I can hear the river, just like he said. And I can picture scenes from the play like it's a movie and Leo's guitar is the music in the background. I close my eyes so this classroom disappears but the music keeps going. I'm mesmerized.

When he finishes, everyone claps. Well, Cory doesn't clap, but he's sitting up now and looking at Leo. Mr. Canning is mega impressed. Leo's nailed an A for sure. I'm glad Leo had a chance to do the project he missed. Maybe teachers know all about Leo's mother and Caroline and his father, who's on the road so much and who doesn't live with them, anyway. And now that I think of all this, I can understand why it would be easy for Leo to write music to fit the river of *Romeo and Juliet*.

I dig into my jacket pocket and curl my fingers around Leo's anger rock. One thing I'm sure of right now is that somehow I have to get him talking to me again. I hate that he's mad at me.

At noon, Jenn is waiting at the lockers.

"Look," I say. "I've got to do something right now so I can't go get lunch. Sorry." Then, because of the look on her face, I add, "It's important."

"Right."

"Let's go tomorrow. If Ronny's still sick." I know it's a mean jab to drop that last bit into the mix, but I'm not in the mood to gloss over reality right now.

"Sure," she says. "Better get moving. There goes Leo."

"Thanks," I say. "I'll explain later. Whatever you're thinking, you're wrong."

She smiles and I'm glad she doesn't seem completely bugged anymore.

When I catch up to Leo, he's already outside. I step right in front of him, which makes him stop. "I need to talk to you. I'm sorry about saying that stuff on Saturday. About how mad you get."

"It's none of your business."

"I know. That's why I'm sorry." So far he's not walking away, and I take that as a good sign and keep on talking. "Sometimes I think of something and just blurt it out before I realize I should keep my mouth shut."

"Exactly," he says.

I realize this conversation needs a quick one-eighty turn. "Your *Romeo and Juliet* river was amazing. I didn't know you wrote music."

"Neither did I," he says.

"I really liked the fight scene with all the anger and confusion, and then how you stopped for, like, two or three seconds before you made the music sound scary."

"It was supposed to mean the guy died."

"That's what I meant."

"I still say Shakespeare's twisted."

"I don't think it'll hurt his feelings."

Leo laughs. Okay, it was more like a snort, but there was definitely humor appreciation involved.

I take a chance and ask, "You going to see Caroline again?"

"Yeah. Saturday."

"If you need someone to keep you from looking like a criminal when you're hitchhiking, I'd go."

"Sure. Maybe."

I don't bug him about the contradiction of saying those two words in the same breath. I'll assume it's a go.

* * *

This time I'm prepared. Wool scarf and mittens. Also a hat that pulls down over my ears. And very warm socks. I don't get all this talk about global warming when it's barely halfway through November and already it's iceberg city.

Leo's wearing a heavy winter jacket with a hood.

Ironically, a guy in an old car pulls over as we're walking up the ramp toward the highway, and we haven't even had a chance to get cold, "Let me guess. You two're about to hitchhike," he says. "Hop in."

Leo starts to get in the front when the guy says, "Girls in front."

"That's okay," I say. I'm a bit creeped.

"Rules are rules," he says.

Leo says, "We'll pass." Then he slams the door and mutters something I don't exactly hear but I can pretty much guess what it was.

The guy takes off with squealing tires and blue smoke.

"Creepy," I say.

"Loser," says Leo.

Eventually, another car stops and this time the guy looks like an ordinary person. No creep vibes. He's going to Yarmouth, so we've scored a drive all the way to exit six.

It takes three more drives before we get from exit six to North West Cove. The last drive is a guy who knows Leo's aunt and the guy she lives with. "They got a little girl stayin' with them, I hear."

"Yeah," says Leo. "My sister."

"Oh. Mm." Right away the guy reads Leo's mind and doesn't ask any questions. "Nice you'd be going to see her."

"Yeah."

It's comfortable in this car. I don't mean the seats or anything. I mean the atmosphere. This man's definitely very nice. Perceptive. Considerate. He drives us all the way to Jane's house where there's a transport truck parked in the driveway. Silver and blue and very shiny. It's only half a transport truck because the big box part isn't on it. Whoever owns this either just bought it or they clean it with a toothbrush after every trip.

"Shit," says Leo, not quite under his breath.

I'm putting two and two together, adding things up to the fact that this truck belongs to Leo's father, because Leo said he was on the road so much. Genius.

"Ah, I don't think Jane's home right now," says Leo. "Mind dropping us off down at the garage?"

When the car pulls away from the garage, we stand there for a second not saying anything. Then I decide there's nothing to lose by stating the obvious. "That was your father's truck at Jane's."

Leo says nothing.

I make another loop around my neck with my scarf.

"Let's go in here for a minute," he says.

Inside the garage it's only slightly warmer. There's a counter where they sell bars and chips and pop. The guy who's been putting cigarettes into a drawer stops and looks at us.

"You want anything?" says Leo.

"No, thanks."

He buys a chocolate bar and we stand inside while he eats it. I can tell he's trying to figure out what to do.

"Maybe he's not actually at your aunt's. Maybe he just left his truck there," I say, trying to be helpful.

The guy behind the counter says, "If you're looking for someone from around here, they're likely at the firemen's breakfast. Pretty well everyone goes. Finishes up about eleven or thereabout."

Leo opens the door and leaves.

"Thanks," I say to the guy behind the counter.

I'm starting to wish I wasn't here. I feel all weird again, like I'm nobody and I'm nowhere and no one knows me. Which in a way is true. I hate when I get this feeling. "So now what're we going to do?" I ask.

"Go back to Jane's."

I don't like the stormy look in Leo's eyes. He's fuming mad about something…probably the fact that his father's around. I don't want to be there when the two of them meet face to face. But what else am I going to do?

Leo walks up the driveway, directly to the transport truck, and goes around the back, where he leans down and looks underneath. He reaches with one hand and hangs on to the back with his other hand. He's holding a key when he straightens up.

"What're you going to do with that?"

"Drive this truck." Leo's obviously thinking up something that's not going to be a good scene. He reaches up, opens the cab door, climbs the two steps, and settles into the driver's seat.

For some idiotic and stupidly dramatic reason, I run around the other side and climb up into the truck too.

"Get out of the truck, Emily," he says quietly.

"No."

"Don't be an idiot."

"Why'm I an idiot? I'm just sitting here in the truck with you while we wait for everyone to come back from that breakfast." My heart's beating extremely fast. I know for certain that the only thing standing between Leo and trouble right now is me.

He sits there, looking out through the windshield.

This truck's so huge I feel like I'm in an airplane, waiting for takeoff.

Leo starts the truck. It sounds like a dozen garbage cans rattling under the hood. For sure no one's home, because by now they'd be running outside to catch whoever's stealing this truck. Can Leo even drive this thing? Don't people need special training and—

"If you're not getting out then put on your seatbelt."

He revs the engine and checks the gages on the dash. Then he pushes on a gear shift and the truck starts moving forward.

"Do you know how to drive this thing?" I snap on the seatbelt.

"It's automatic. Anyone can drive one of these. It's not rocket science."

"But this is humongous! Look at all these buttons and stuff. It's not an ordinary truck!" I'm getting a bit hysterical.

Leo stops the truck. "If you want to, you can get out."

"Where are you going? What if your father sees us in his truck?"

"Last chance if you wanna get out."

"I'm not getting out." I try to calm down my hysteria. Not that I know him very well, but I have a feeling Leo won't do anything entirely stupid with me here in this truck with him.

We rumble along the windy road past the garage, then down around a sharp curve at the end of the cove, and then up a very steep hill. Leo's driving slowly and smoothly, so I try to relax a bit. I can see way out over the cove from up here. All those wharves and boats and lopsided fishing shacks. Like a postcard.

I'm getting used to driving along in this truck, but I'm relieved when we're past the houses in the cove and away from any chances of Leo's father seeing his truck go by. "So where're we going?"

"Dunno."

"Not on the main highway, okay?"

"I don't plan to go that far. I'm not an idiot." He's watching the road and leaning his long arms on the steering wheel like he's driven this truck lots of times before.

We drive for about twenty minutes and come to a small picnic park beside a rocky beach. Leo pulls off the road and stops the truck.

"Now what?" I say.

He pulls on the emergency brake but he doesn't turn off the engine. "Let's hitchhike back home."

"What? And just leave your father's truck here?"

"Yeah."

"But—"

Leo's already getting out.

"Are you just leaving the truck running like this? With the keys in the ignition?" I jump down from the truck and follow him back to the side of the road.

"That's the plan."

"Why?"

"Because it'll piss my father off when he eventually finds his precious truck. And if I'm lucky, it'll be out of fuel and that'll piss him off even more."

"He'll know you did this."

"Who cares?"

"What if someone comes along and sees the truck running and takes it?"

"Everyone on this road knows the truck's Dad's. They wouldn't touch it. Come on. Let's get going."

What choice do I have?

Seven

It didn't take us long to get back to the city. I was tired and cold and extremely worried about how Leo abandoned his father's truck like that. It's going to mean big trouble. And not just for Leo, either.

Saturday night and all I want is to stay in my room alone. Mom and Dad are watching a movie, which in other circumstances I might watch with them, but no way could I concentrate on a movie tonight.

Leo's father's bound to find his truck and know who took it and the exact reason why. I picture his father being an older version of Leo. Maybe even bigger. When Leo says his father's an idiot, it might just be another way of saying the man has anger issues. The same ones Leo inherited.

And Caroline's so little and so sweet. I remember how Leo said, "Ping-Pong anyone?" when Jane told him that Caroline would live sometimes with her dad and sometimes with Jane. Now I have this ominous feeling that what Leo did today is somehow going to make things a lot worse for Caroline. Maybe his father will try to keep Leo from visiting her. Can he legally do that?

This is when I suddenly think of Aunt Em. I won't call her tonight because it's ten-thirty, and calling now would make this situation more into an emergency when I really want to tone everything down. But tomorrow I'll call and find out from her exactly what could happen to Leo police-wise and court-wise. And what could potentially happen to me.

I can't sleep.

Even after reading almost three chapters of this book, which I can't remember anything about, I'm not the least bit sleepy. Mom went to bed at least two hours ago and Dad went not long after that. I go to the washroom very quietly. There's no light showing under their bedroom door, which means they're probably asleep.

I look out my bedroom window and wonder whether Leo's father found his truck yet.

It's 1:20.

Even though I know it's not necessarily a good idea, considering what happened last week, I decide to go out again. It's cold, but not freezing cold. I wear my scarf and mittens anyway.

I close our front door and stand for a minute facing the street, almost thinking I should just turn around and go right back inside. It's crazy to go for a walk when everyone else is in bed sleeping. I know it's crazy. And it probably isn't safe. Why would I keep doing something that probably isn't safe?

For sure I'm not going the way I went last time. The more traffic, the more likely there's losers around, so I keep to quiet streets.

I should be afraid. But it's all how you look at it. If this was two o'clock in the afternoon, I'd be walking anywhere I wanted and who'd care? And people feel safe on their own streets. Just take that to the extreme and all neighborhoods must be safe because there's people in every neighborhood who aren't afraid to be there because that's where they live. So that means I don't have to be afraid, no matter what street I'm walking on.

It's a darkness-and-shadows night. Quiet. I actually like this. Being away from everybody and just walking by myself. I don't even have to think about anything if I don't want to. I'm here. I'm me. That's it.

When I decide to go back home, I'm just walking at my normal pace. I'm not afraid because what's there to be afraid of, anyway.

* * *

Leo's ahead of me. I'm hurrying a bit so I can tell him what I need to tell him.

Some guys are razzing a girl who's a few steps in front of Leo. "Don't turn around. Don't turn around," one of them is saying to her. "Don't say hi. Don't say hi."

She doesn't turn around and she doesn't say hi. As she opens the door, Leo grabs it and holds it for her. I slow down, partly out of amazement because I just saw the look on Leo's face.

He doesn't notice me, even when we're inside.

"Hey," says Leo, "that was cool. I said that was cool. Out there. How you just kept—Hey, what's the hurry?"

The girl stops and turns around. "Huh? What?"

"I said it was cool what you did out there. You just ignored those guys. Like they didn't exist."

"One of them's my cousin," she says. "Just showing off."

I've stopped a few steps behind Leo. Like I'm spying, but I'm not. I just need to tell him what I need to tell him. The main hall's crowded with people coming in through the front doors and heading in all directions.

"What's your instrument?" I hear Leo ask.

The girl's carrying a narrow black case. She looks down at it. "Flute."

"Cool."

"Look," she says in a kind of distracted way, "I gotta get to class." It's obvious she's not sure why this guy she doesn't know is talking to her.

As she walks away, Leo says, "Hey! I'm Leo. Hey, what's your name?"

She doesn't turn around but he keeps watching her walk away, carrying the flute and her overstuffed backpack covered in buttons of all colors and sizes. Her long brown hair hangs down past her shoulders. She's wearing jeans, very tight jeans which—and I'm not being critical—are tight because she has quite a bit of extra weight. I didn't get a good look at her face because of Leo being in the way and because she left so fast.

I'm pretty sure I just witnessed Leo falling in love. Amazing! Before he has a chance to know that I've been standing here the whole time, I turn around and disappear.

I make a plan to corner him at break so we can have a conversation about his father's truck. And this time he can't say it's none of my business. It definitely is my business because I was there too.

Last night I called Aunt Em to ask her about what's likely to happen after the truck is found and his father figures out who took it. I told the whole thing straight, just as if I was one of her clients. Every detail. Her pro-

fession kicked in and her voice sounded like a lawyer
and not like an aunt. She asked me questions and listened very carefully to everything I said. I was glad I
couldn't see her face. It made it much easier. I know
she wasn't shocked because she's had cases way worse
than this. But I am her niece, so it must've been weird
hearing me tell her all that stuff that she probably never
thought I could be involved in.

"The good news," she said, "is Leo's father might
not report the truck missing." But I told her there was
fat chance for that because of how his father's supposed
to be an idiot, which Aunt Em reminded me is hearsay.
The part I need to explain to Leo is that once his father
reports his truck stolen, and even if he says it was his
son, the Mounties will charge Leo with theft. Aunt Em
said that no one can change their mind and say, well,
it's okay and we forgive him this time, or anything like
that because it'll be in the hands of the Mounties. If by a
long shot his father doesn't say his truck was stolen, Leo
could get charged with joyriding, and even that's big
trouble. He's over eighteen, which means adult court.

I was in that truck too. The worst-case scenario for
me, even though Aunt Em said it's highly unlikely, is that
I get charged with theft too. As long as Leo says I tried
to stop him, which I sort of did, then I won't be charged.
Aunt Em said I have to tell Mom and Dad ASAP, in case

the Mounties knock on our door and inform them that I was involved in joyriding or even possibly theft. But I haven't told them yet.

This whole thing is making me crazy. Crazier.

I rush like mad out of math class, but I'm too late. There's Leo and he's talking to the flute player again. I can't believe how cool and collected he's acting right now when he's potentially in mega trouble up to his eyeballs. I'm a wreck.

Surprise, surprise. The girl is walking away. Again. He's soon going to have to take the hint. But I don't have time to think about Leo's love life right now.

"I have to talk to you."

Leo turns around and stands there, looking down at me.

"Last night I called my Aunt Em who's a legal aid lawyer and asked her about what could happen because of your father's truck."

"How much'd you tell her?"

"Everything."

"What'd you do that for?"

"Because we're potentially in a pile of trouble!"

"No, we're not."

"What do you mean?"

"Dad wasn't around. He's hunting in Newfoundland. He left his truck at Jane's while he's away."

"When did you find all this out?"

"Saturday. I called Jane to tell her where the truck was. So she drove Dan over to get it—I told her it might be out of fuel—and he drove it back to her place. End of story."

"Thanks for keeping me informed." I sound snarky and I don't care. "What if someone saw us and told your dad?"

"That's not gonna happen."

"Right," I say sarcastically.

"Unless your aunt spills the beans. Better tell her the problem's solved."

"Yeah," I say, and suddenly I feel almost relieved. I won't have to explain all this to Mom and Dad because there's really nothing to explain. "Won't Jane say anything about this to him?"

"She knows that'd be like lighting the fuse on a time bomb. But she says now I have to call her every morning before I head for school, and every night when I get back home. Like probation." Then he says, "Mom's in rehab again."

"Oh." I can't tell if he thinks this will be a good thing for his mother or not. Probably there's a pattern here that Leo knows like the back of his hand.

I want to make it sound like my mind has switched lanes completely, so I brighten my voice up a bit and say, "How about coming to my place and hang out after school?"

"Maybe," he says with this cautious look.

After school Leo says he wants to go over to his place and get his guitar, so I go with him. His bus stop's only two past mine. He lives in a building that has four apartments and his is number three. Second floor. When he opens the apartment door, I step inside and just wait while he goes to get his guitar down the hallway somewhere. I can see the living room couch, and I think of his mom passed out there with Caroline needing someone to help her get ready for school. The fact that Leo's living here alone is a bit depressing, even though maybe it's calmer without his mother passed out every day.

When we get to my place, Mom's face is full of question marks and I can't say I blame her. She puts the TV on mute and stands up.

"Mom, this is my friend, Leo Mac." *Who's a truck thief and has anger issues and an idiot father and an alcoholic mother and this very sweet little sister.* "Leo, this is Mom."

"Hi," says Leo.

"Nice to meet you," says Mom in a very motherly voice.

"We're gonna hang out in my room for a while."

"Would you like something to eat?"

"You want something?" I ask Leo.

"Coffee, if it's okay." He's very soft right now. And it's not phony. I half expect him to tell Mom that I'm not his type so she can relax about why he's here.

"I'll make coffee," I say, and we head for the kitchen. I hear the TV when Mom turns off the mute.

Out of all the music I've got, Leo likes just this one CD so we play it a couple of times, and he quietly strums his guitar with most of the songs. I don't feel strange at all, being here in my room listening to Leo play guitar. It's peaceful.

"My grandmother died in a car accident." I blurt this out almost before I know I'm thinking about it.

Leo stops strumming the guitar and just stares at me.

"I don't know what made me think about that."

"When'd it happen?"

"A long time ago. Dad and Aunt Em were only five."

I tell Leo about Granddad's affair with Cynthia Maxwell and how that probably ended up causing my grandmother's accident. Then I tell about his daughter who doesn't know she's his daughter. Leo listens. Really listens.

"That's twisted," he says when I finish. "Sorry. But it is. Your family's just as screwed up as mine."

That sort of hurts my feelings. I don't think Mom and Dad or Aunt Em are screwed up. It's basically just

Granddad. But right now I don't want to argue about whose family is screwed up and whose isn't. It'll ruin everything.

We hear Dad's car in the driveway. "Dad's home," I say.

"I gotta go," says Leo, "or your mother'll invite me to supper with your screwed-up family."

"Very funny."

"It was okay hangin' with you," he says when he's packing up his guitar.

"Yeah. You too."

If someone had told me a few weeks ago that I'd have this guy for a friend, hanging out here in my room, hitchhiking together in the freezing cold, telling each other stuff about mothers or grandmothers, I would've thought they'd lost it. For a second I consider why I haven't mentioned anything to Leo about Brian. But instantly I picture his reaction. He'd tell me how it was lame wasting time on someone who's already moved on. He'd probably be right.

When Mom and Dad and I are having supper, Mom asks, "Why didn't you invite your friend for supper?"

"Maybe next time," I say.

"Seems like a nice enough guy," says Dad.

I give Dad a sideways look to see if remembers what I told him about Leo being just a friend or if he's jumping to any romantic conclusions. But he's concentrating on mashing butter into his potatoes. When he finishes that, I know he'll want the salt and pepper, so I put them beside him.

Mom looks at how much salt he shakes on his potatoes, but she doesn't say anything this time.

When I was a little kid and wouldn't eat my vegetables, Dad would mash my potatoes and smooth them flat on my plate with his knife. Then he'd spread butter in a very thin layer across the top. He'd carve even rows up and down and side to side, creating a grid of buttered potato squares. Then, one by one, he'd lift up those squares with my fork and offer them to me like a special treasure. I'd eat the whole grid that way. Sometimes eating isn't about the food.

After supper I'll call Aunt Em to let her know that the pressure's off about Leo's father's truck. I'm not going to bother telling Mom and Dad anything about it now that it's a non-story. Maybe someday, like when I'm twenty or something, and we're sitting around talking about old times, I'll tell them about the day Leo and I took a ride in his father's 18-wheeler and left it at a picnic park. I can picture Mom, biting her lip and worrying like crazy about something that happened so long ago. Dad'll probably say he's glad he didn't know about all the trouble his little girl was getting into, and I'll be thinking that I'm glad he didn't too.

Before I get a chance to call Aunt Em, she calls us. Dad answers the phone. Obviously she has something important to tell him because he gets quiet after he says hi. I'm hoping she isn't saying anything about Leo's father's truck, assuming I would've told Mom and Dad by now.

Then Dad says, "You're kidding."

He listens some more while Mom and I watch him standing there with his back to us.

"So when'd she find out?" He turns around and looks at us. "Sure. We're just finishing supper. Okay." He hangs up the phone.

I'm thinking, *When did who find out what?* but I don't say anything.

"Emma's coming over. She says that Cynthia Maxwell's daughter flew in from Toronto and phoned her just now."

"Her daughter's here?" says Mom, probably thinking like I'm thinking that Mrs. Maxwell said her daughter didn't know about Granddad and definitely not about any of us, either, so how come she'd show up here?

"She knows Dad was her father. Now she wants to meet us. Tomorrow sometime."

The plot thickens.

When Aunt Em gets here, she tells us that Cynthia

Maxwell's daughter's married and works for some supposedly well-known magazine that none of us ever heard of. Dana is her name. "Pronounced Dan-a," says Aunt Em.

Mom says tomorrow we'll have dinner together here, and she'll make lasagna with no meat because, according to Aunt Em, Dana's a vegetarian. I like Mom's spinach and mushroom lasagna better than meat lasagna, anyway.

Wonder what Cynthia Maxwell's thinking now that her big secret's not a secret anymore.

Eight

Not that I have a problem with it or anything like that, but I really wasn't expecting Dana to be married to a woman. And I know for certain that Mom and Dad and Aunt Em are trying not to have totally stunned looks on their faces right now. Which makes us all seem like we live in the dark ages.

Dana's calm and cool. Like she doesn't even notice our stunned faces. She's thrilled to be at this family reunion. "I'm Dana," she says with this big smile. "And this is Myra."

"I'm Gerald. Gerry," says Dad. "And this is Emma. And my wife Winnie. And Emily."

Everyone says hi but no one hugs. It's weird. Awkward. Like Granddad's standing right here in the middle of this family group saying, *Over my dead body*.

"Let me take your coats," says Dad.

We go into the living room where there's a fire in the fireplace and candles lit on the coffee table.

"It gets dark so early this time of year," says Mom, maybe to explain the candles, but probably just to fill up the empty air space all around us.

"And it's not usually this cold in November," says Aunt Em.

What would people do if they didn't have weather to talk about at times like this? When we're all thinking private and confusing things, like whether Granddad ever met Dana and if he knew she's a lesbian who's married or whether Dana had a clue that her mother was having an affair with a married man for almost a quarter of a century.

Myra sits on the sofa and Dana sits beside her. They make a nice couple. Myra's about the same height as Dana, but Dana is quite a bit bigger. Dana's hair is very short. Myra's hair is flying all over the place with natural-looking curls. It gives her a kind of whimsical look. I can't picture her being unhappy. She has a glittery purple scarf with braided fringes and a soft green sweater. Dana's wearing jeans and a white T-shirt under a black V-neck sweater. Basic.

"I like your earrings," I say to Myra. They're dangly purple earrings shaped like tropical fish.

She tucks a mass of curls behind one ear and says,

"Dana bought them today at a sweet little craft shop down at the harbor front."

"Historic Properties," says Dana. She smiles and puts her hand on Myra's knee and leaves it there.

Dana doesn't look much like Dad and Aunt Em. More like what Cynthia Maxwell would've looked like when she was in her thirties.

"Well," says Dad.

"You got that right," says Dana and laughs. "Mom's not too happy about me coming here, as you might expect. But you already know she's not into transparency." She gives another laugh. "In a way I'm glad Dad passed away before all this floated up to the surface," she says. "He definitely believed I was his daughter, always saying how much I looked like the portrait of his mother. There actually is some resemblance, too." Another laugh. "You would've liked Dad. Easygoing. Kind."

I expect Mom to say that this man was the opposite of Granddad, but she gets up and says, "I'll leave you to your conversation while I do some last-minute dinner preparations."

"May I help?" asks Myra, already standing up.

"No, dear. You relax."

"Preparing food is relaxing," she says, and follows Mom into the kitchen.

I'm not going anywhere.

Dad and Aunt Em look at each other and then at me.

"I'm okay with Emily here," says Dana, picking up on their vibe. "We're all family. And I'm not about to repeat the secrecy scenario that Mom and Karl were into. What's the point?"

Over my dead body, I hear again, like Granddad's sitting in that chair where he always sat, fuming about all three of his kids being here in the same room for the very first time.

So Aunt Em and Dad tell Dana about Meredith marrying Granddad when they were barely six years old and how she's at Harmony Hills now and doesn't understand that he died. They don't go into detail about the possible cause of the car accident, and I get that. Why give Dana something to feel bad about right now when she's so happy being here with us?

"We don't remember a lot about our mother. Just impressions and foggy memories," says Aunt Em with a small smile. A melancholy smile.

They also tell about Granddad's insurance business and how he expanded and moved to Victoria Street, and that Dad owns the company now. But I notice they don't say anything about all those affair conferences Granddad went to for twenty-three years. They're sticking to the censored version of things.

Dad makes a joke about marrying Mom because he didn't know how to cook. He looks over at me and says, "Then Emily came along and nothing's been the same since."

"He means that in a good way," I say.

"When I look at you three, I see such a strong family resemblance. Wonderful," says Dana.

Dad and Aunt Em are smiling at me, which makes me all self-conscious.

Dana tells us that she and Myra got married six years ago. Her mother wouldn't come to the wedding, but her father did. He said he was proud to see her marry such a fine person as Myra. Myra's parents were at the wedding and her brother and some cousins. "And, of course, all our friends," she says.

I'm thinking she was lucky to have the father she had instead of her real father. *Birth father*, she calls Granddad.

"Mom eventually got over it," she says. "We do lots of things together, especially since Dad died. Myra and I sometimes drive over to Montreal and we go to the symphony together. Or she comes to Toronto and we take her to musicals and shopping. She spends Christmas with us now."

I'm listening to this but I'm starting to think about

Brian because of Montreal and Christmas being topics of discussion. I know for a fact that as long as he's not around, it's easier.

"Let's go see if the table's set, Emily," says Aunt Em. And I get the hint that it might be good for Dad and Dana to have a few minutes to talk alone.

During dinner we're all gabbing as if we've known each other for ages. Dana and Myra just got back from Paris where they go every year because that's where they had their honeymoon. They ask me about school, and I say that soon there'll be just one more semester left before I graduate. And when I tell them I'm planning to get a biology degree or a history degree but I don't exactly know what I want to do profession-wise, they don't act like I'm a misguided, directionless teenager like the counselors at school do. Aunt Em tells a few funny stories about clients, without saying their actual names, of course. All the while everyone keeps telling Mom that her lasagna is just the best, which it is. Myra asks Mom to email the recipe and she says she will.

They're staying at a B&B downtown and Aunt Em offers to drive them there.

"I guess this is the kind of thing sisters do for each other," says Dana.

The way she says this makes us get all quiet, standing together there in the front hall.

"Brothers too," says Aunt Em, smiling at Dad.

"I like having another aunt," I say.

"Another two aunts," Dana says, taking Myra's hand and giving me one of those calm and comfortable smiles.

Later, Aunt Em and I put dishes in the dishwasher. Mom and Dad watch TV together, probably debriefing. Wonder what Mom's saying about all this.

"So what's it like having a sister?"

"It doesn't quite seem real," says Aunt Em.

"Does to Dana. You can tell."

"I'm so used to it being just Gerry and me. Twins are in their own world. It's got something to do with sharing the same womb and being born minutes apart."

I'm mesmerized by what I'm imagining. Two tadpole babies floating together for months. Bumping into each other. Squinting through their watery world to get a closer look. Until something clicks and they're pushing their way out. "Who was born first, you or Dad?"

"Me. By three minutes."

"I think it'd be cool to have a brother or a sister." I think of Caroline and Leo. How much she counts on him. How having a little sister keeps Leo from floating away like a balloon without a string. "Wonder why Mom and Dad only had me."

Aunt Em suddenly gets this look on her face and I

know she's about to say something serious. "Winnie had a baby, Emily. A boy. It was stillborn."

This stuns me.

She looks over her shoulder as if somehow Mom could hear us. "I shouldn't have told you that."

"Why don't I already know?"

Aunt Em looks toward the hallway again and then back at me. "I think eventually they'd tell you."

"I'm not a kid. I understand about stillborn babies." I'm miffed.

"I don't want you to let on that you know."

"Oh, great. Now you're just like Granddad."

"It's not like that, Emily."

"It is like that!" I didn't mean to raise my voice so much.

"What are you two disagreeing about?" Mom's carrying two empty teacups. She looks very relaxed, so I'm thinking the debriefing was a good thing.

"Nothing, really." I take the cups from Mom. I want to tell her I know about her stillborn baby. I want to tell her I understand.

"Thanks, dear," says Mom as I put the cups in the top rack.

When I'm in bed, I can't sleep. I'm trying to picture Dad and Mom and their stillborn baby. Did they get to hold him? Did they have a name picked out?

Then I think about Leo, who's by himself right now with his idiot father somewhere in Newfoundland and his mother in rehab and his sweet little sister Caroline, curled up sleeping at Jane's in a bed that's not even hers. Probably Leo's having a hard time getting to sleep too.

"What's the difference? It's got nothing to do with you, anyway. It happened before you were even born."

When I told Leo about Dana and Myra, he just said, "Whatever." But then, for some illogical and highly emotional reason, I go and tell him about Mom's still-born baby, and how no one told me about him until Aunt Em let it slip last night.

"It's got everything to do with me. It's my father and my mother and he would've been my brother."

"Would've been but isn't."

"You don't have emotions."

"I don't waste emotions."

Just past Leo's shoulder I see the girl with the flute coming into the cafeteria. Speaking of wasting emotions. She's looking around and when she doesn't find whoever it is she's looking for, she leaves.

"What?" he says, looking over his shoulder because it's obvious I've been watching someone.

"Not what. Who."

"Then, who?"

"The girl with the flute. She was just here, but she left."

He gives me this look. "Mind your own business."

"Touchy," I say in an exaggerated way.

He grabs his milk carton and sandwich wrap and stands up. "Gotta go."

"She turned right."

He pretends he doesn't hear this, but I know he did because when he leaves the cafeteria, he turns right.

"Emily!" It's Jenn, with Ronny beside her. "Where's your man?"

"Funny," I say.

They sit down across from me. Now I'll look totally ignorant if I get up and leave.

Jenn grins like there hasn't been a bump in our friendship. Ronny starts to fill his face with hamburger and fries.

"We should do something sometime," says Jenn.

"Meaning?"

"The four of us. A movie or something."

Ronny doesn't respond to this idea. He's looking off into nowhere as if chewing food's a complicated job.

"We're not dating."

"I say give this new guy a chance."

"You're not listening."

Ronny looks over at me with one cheek stuffed with food. He wasn't listening either. It's like two blank walls are sitting across from me.

I get up and leave, figuring the blank walls won't realize that I'm being totally rude.

Leo and the flute player are on the stairs. She's a couple of steps above him so he's looking up at her which must be weird because he's used to being the one looking down. I stop so I don't mess things up by walking past them. But the flute player looks directly at me and gets this very uptight expression on her face. I know exactly what she's thinking and she's 100 percent wrong. She cuts off the conversation with Leo and hurries up the stairs.

Leo doesn't move.

"She's jumping to conclusions," I say when I'm standing beside him.

I don't bother telling him that the flute player isn't the only person at this school who's jumping to conclusions. Be fun, though, to see the look on his face if I told him about Barbie's plan for us to double-date with her and Ken. "And don't tell me to mind my own business again."

"Come with me, then," he says.

"What?"

"If you're not there, she won't believe me."

Right.

When we get to the top of the stairs, the flute player's down the hall, talking to a couple of guys. One of them's holding a tuba like he's in the middle of a rehearsal.

"Shouldn't we wait till she's by herself?" I'm not liking the very awkward scene that's playing out in my mind.

"No time," says Leo.

I haven't quite caught up to him when he gets to the flute player.

"It's not what you think," says Leo. "Emily, tell her it's not what she thinks."

A bit of preamble might've been a better strategy, I'm thinking. They're all waiting for me to speak, so I follow Leo's tactic and jump right in. "Leo and I are friends. Not boyfriend-girlfriend."

No one says anything.

I look at Leo. He's waiting for me to keep going.

"Just now, when you were talking to Leo, you saw me coming and you took off like I'd be mad. Of course I'm not mad because there's no reason to be mad."

Leo looks satisfied with this.

But I can't resist. "Leo can have the hots for who-ever he wants to have the hots for, and it's none of my business."

The tuba player leans to the mouthpiece and blows three elephant groans.

The only ones not grinning now are Leo and the flute player. He can't believe that I just said what I said. And she's connecting all the dots.

Time for a dramatic exit.

As I'm walking away, I'm grinning. I love razzing Leo like that. The look on his face! If I had a brother I'd want him to be exactly like Leo.

Immediately I'm thinking about Mom's stillborn baby. If that little baby boy had lived, I would've had an older brother. All my life I would've had an older brother.

The smell of peanut butter cookies is all through the house. I love peanut butter cookies the way Mom makes them. Huge and chewy.

"Don't spoil your supper," she says when I take one from the cooling rack.

I lean against the counter as she takes another pan of cookies out of the oven. I'm still thinking about what it would've been like, having an older brother. I think he'd be the teasing type, dancing Mom all around the kitchen and singing an opera about peanut butter cookies. She'd be telling him to stop but she'd be laughing. And when they stopped dancing around, I'd be clapping and saying, "Bravo!" Mom would have to take a corner of her apron and wipe the laughing tears out of her eyes.

"You look like the cat that swallowed a canary," says Mom.

I don't want her to know that I know about her stillborn baby, so I fake what I'm thinking about and tell her about Leo and the flute player and how I announced that Leo has the hots for her.

"She would have had that all figured out," says Mom. "Women are always ahead of men that way."

"Maybe she already likes some other guy."

"Then she would have come right out and told your friend that she has a boyfriend."

"Maybe she thinks Leo's a stalker."

"Oh, I don't think so. Especially if she's seen him with you."

"Right. Not exactly stalker profile."

"I think he's a very nice boy. Just something about him that you notice as soon as you meet him."

"I hope she gives him a chance." I tell Mom about how Leo's living by himself now, and all about his mother and his father and Caroline. "Then teachers go and say he's got anger issues when who wouldn't have anger issues if all that stuff was happening in their lives. Leo's a funny guy in a low-key way. You just have to pay attention."

"And you're not interested in him? As a boyfriend?"

"He's like a brother." The words are out before I realize what I've said.

But Mom's on another wavelength. "Do you think he'd like it if I packed up some cookies for him?"

"Sure," I say. "I'll take them to school tomorrow."

That's Mom for you. Got a problem? Good home cooking's the answer. But I don't tease her about this because, in Leo's case, she's probably right.

I grab another cookie and Mom pretends to smack my hand away.

"Dana and Myra called from the airport to say how much they enjoyed our dinner. Meeting all of us. They went to visit Meredith this morning and brought her flowers."

"She wouldn't get who they were."

"No, but that's not the point. It was very nice of them to visit her."

I put Leo's container of cookies in my backpack so I won't forget them tomorrow. "I really, really like Dana and Myra," I say.

"Impossible not to," says Mom.

Nine

It's snowing and it's December, so I get this idea to make a Christmas card for Brian. I'm not naïve enough to think anything like a Christmas card'll change the way things are, but I want to make a statement. Not in words. A symbolic statement. Basically to make him feel bad.

So I've taken the chopped-up pictures out of my photo album and they're lying all over my bed. Me without Brian at the beach. Me without Brian at a Valentine's dance. Me without Brian standing beside half of Jenn's car. Me without Brian having a snowball fight. Me without Brian sitting on our front steps. Me playing with Brian's dog while no one holds the leash. I thought I had a picture of us (me) in front of a Christmas tree, but I can't find it.

And I'm fighting a gigantic feeling that this whole

idea is probably majorly immature. It's like I'm a little kid going downhill on my tricycle with my feet off the pedals.

Folding this construction paper in half reminds me of how I always made Christmas cards for Mom and Dad and Aunt Em and Granddad and Meredith. Little cards with candles or holly or bells cut from old Christmas cards glued on the front and with my lopsided printing inside.

Brian's card's not really a Christmas card.

The construction paper is black. Obvious, but I don't care. The sliced-up photos will look great on black. I want the whole inside to be a collage of me without Brian.

When all the pictures are glued on, I can't think of what to write on the outside. *Have a Merry Christmas* might not come across in the sarcastic, insincere way I want it to. But then I think that writing it on black paper is equal to sarcasm and insincerity, so I pick up the glue again and squeeze out the letters like putting icing words on a cake. I sprinkle the gluey letters with purple glitter. After a few seconds I shake the extra glitter off.

I hold the card and think about Brian holding it. *Have a Merry Xmas*. No exclamation mark. Bits of purple glitter fall across my thumb as I open the card. There I am, tilted sideways, standing straight, upside down, and horizontal. Me, me, me, me, me, me, me.

This is pathetic. I'm not going to mail this card.

I put away all the scattered pictures and brush glitter off the bedspread. I think of throwing the card away, but instead I put it inside one of my textbooks.

I sit back and go over in my mind what I've just been up to for the last hour. I look around and think about how this is the same bed and the same bedroom and the same curtains and most of the same pictures on the wall that I've had forever. The only thing that's really different since I was a little kid is that my desk is bigger. And there aren't any crayons. Okay, the books are different too. And the CDs. And my laptop. But the point is that right now I feel like I'm that same little kid when, really, I'm supposed to be almost an adult. What adult would send a black Christmas card with a self-portrait collage to their former boyfriend? A sicko, simpering, self-centered person who needs to get a grip.

Very depressing.

I hear Dad shoveling the back steps. It's still snowing, but he likes to keep ahead of the piling-up snow, although it always piles right back up as fast as he can shovel it.

When I get outside, he says, "I was wondering when you'd be coming out."

I grab the other shovel and slice into a drift. I like

being out here at night with the lights from the shed and the back door swirling with snow. The wind comes around the shed and blows across the top of the car. You have to make sure you throw the snow with the wind and not at it, although I don't always remember this.

When the snowplow comes along, we both wave at the driver. Dad says it helps to be out there shoveling when the plow goes by because then the guy isn't likely to dump a load of snow at the bottom of our driveway. Once, when I was maybe seven, we had a major blizzard that shut everything down for a couple days, and Dad took a drink of rum out to the plow guy when he came down our street for the hundredth time.

I'm frozen and my feet are wet and my nose is running a marathon by the time we go back in the house. But I'm not depressed anymore.

School's cancelled. It's the most perfect sunny day with no wind and with everything coated in white, white, white.

When we finish (again) shoveling the driveway and the walkway to our front door and along the sidewalk to where our neighbors stopped shoveling, I ask Dad for one of those brown business envelopes. It's actually too big, but I don't care. And even though there'll probably be no mail pickup today, I walk to the end of our block and mail Brian's Xmas card so it'll be at his house whenever he gets home for the holidays. After I thought about it last night, I decided that sending this card isn't really sicko. Just a poignant reminder of a relationship past. Sort of like those ghost nightmares Scrooge has because he's been such a crappy person.

Big surprise. Leo's eating lunch with the flute player.

I forget about the three's-a-crowd rule and sit down across from them because I'm very curious about what's up with these two. "Hi."

Leo looks like he forgets who I am.

The flute player smiles.

"I'm Emily."

"I'm Sam. Hi." She doesn't look uptight about me being here. Things've obviously been progressing in Leo's love quest.

Her flute case is on a chair and Leo's guitar is leaning against the table. I've been wondering since this morning why he brought his guitar to school. When I sat beside him on the bus and said, "What's with the guitar?" he acted like he didn't hear me because of how noisy it was when the bus took off.

So I try again. "You don't usually bring your guitar to school." Then I turn to Sam. "Except for this English project where he played a music version of *Romeo and Juliet* being a river. He wrote the whole thing. It was awesome."

For sure I just scored points for Leo because Sam's giving him that look.

"We start rehearsing the musical this afternoon," she says.

Leo shifts in his chair. Classic self-conscious squirm.

Oh, so Leo's playing in the musical. Smart move, romance-wise. I decide not to take that any further. "Cool," is all I say.

All of a sudden, there's Brian walking into the cafeteria.

My whole body feels like a waterfall is crashing down over me. I try twice before I can swallow the chunk of sandwich in my mouth.

Leo knows I'm panicking. "What?" he says.

Sam's looking at me too.

"Someone I used to know just walked in," I say.

I can't let Brian see me.

The way he's standing there looking around says he doesn't go to this high school anymore. He's out in the big world. A few guys walk over and start talking to him. Maybe I can escape now.

"I'll see you guys," I say, stuffing my sandwich back in the wrapper.

"Need company?"

This stops me in my tracks. Leo's not joking. He means it.

"Okay," I say.

"I'll check you after school," Sam says to Leo. She's just saying it. No sarcasm. No jealousy.

I really, really must look awful.

I walk slowly, like it's no big deal.

Brian's still talking to those guys and his back's to us. As we walk past, I think I hear him say, "Yeah, right."

"Thanks," I say when we're finally out in the hall. My knees are actually shaking.

"Let's take a walk," says Leo.

We pass the library and keep on going to the very end of the hall, where a bunch of people are sitting on the floor under the stairwell. I go up to the landing and stop at the window. Leo's right beside me.

I hate how cold I feel.

"Who's that guy back there?"

No point faking with Leo. "He used to be my boyfriend…"

He just stands there, waiting, so I say, "Now he has a girlfriend he met at university."

"And you're hoping he'll smarten up and come back to you?" He's trying not to make it sound like I'm some kind of idiot if I actually am hoping he'll come back.

"Not exactly."

"This explains things."

"What things?"

"Like, why you're single."

"I don't think of myself as single," I say. "It's more like me without Brian." Then it clicks. "Ohmygawd!"

"What?"

"Something I did. Something really really really stupid."

I tell him about Brian's Xmas card and this cracks him up.

"But I mailed it!"

"Who cares?"

"I'll look like an idiot."

"No, you won't. Listen," he says. "Go back there. Walk past the guy, say hi, and just keep going. Real casual, like nothing's wrong. He'll be, like, *What's with Emily*? Then he gets the card and the message is loud and clear. You cut him out. Snip snip snip."

"No way I'm going back there."

"Look, I know how a lotta guys think. I'm telling you. I bet he's contemplating cheating on his new girl-friend with you while he's home for Christmas."

It takes a few seconds for that to sink in. I'm looking at Leo and he's looking at me. I play the whole scenario all the way through. Even the part about Brian cheating on his new girlfriend. With me. "Okay. I'll do it."

"This'll be good." Leo's already a couple steps ahead of me.

Just before I get to the cafeteria, I lose my nerve and stop. If Brian's still talking to those guys, maybe he won't even hear me say hi. Or what if he grabs my arm before I get past, and then there's his hand on my arm? I won't be able to handle that. "I can't do it."

"You can so," says Leo, and gives me a shove.

There's Brian. There's the guys he's still talking to. My smile's all wobbly as I walk toward them. Brian sees me. "Oh, hi," I say, barely looking at him. Then, just like that, I'm past him and I keep on going.

When I sit down by Sam, I feel like I just missed getting hit by a tidal wave. "Ohmygawd!" I say. "That was crazy!"

"But fun," says Leo. "Am I right? Am I right?"

"Should I even ask what this is about?" says Sam.

"Wait'll she calms down. She'll tell you. Oh, that was good. So smooth."

"Is he still there? I don't want to turn around."

"Yeah," says Leo. "Wait. No. He's walking away from those guys. Now he's in the hall and heading straight for the main doors. He's gone."

"Okay, Emily," says Sam. "Explain."

* * *

"Brian's home from Montreal already. Ronny saw him here." Jenn's at her locker and Ronny's with her. I don't want to be mean since Jenn's my used-to-be best friend, but I can definitely see she's enjoying the potential for drama.

"Yeah. I saw him too." I take a bit longer getting stuff out of my locker.

"So?"

"So nothing."

"Didn't you talk to him?"

"Just said hi, that's all."

"What's with that?"

"Brian's not my boyfriend anymore, remember? You were the one trying to set me up with a replacement." A nasty dig since the replacement she had in mind is standing right there behind her.

"You don't need to get all sarcastic." Jenn shuts her locker.

I get the feeling she's waiting for me to apologize. I should apologize. Jenn's just being Jenn. A month ago I'd be filling her in on my boring life and she'd be mesmerized by every irrelevant detail.

But I don't say anything.

They walk away. Jenn takes Ronny's hand and I watch them, thinking about predictable endings to bad movies.

* * *

Of course, Leo's not on the bus after school because of practicing for the musical. I wish he was here so I could tell him that what he did today was a big deal. Very big. I feel so different. Not exactly in control, but not out of control, either.

I stay on the bus when it gets to my stop because I've decided to go visit Meredith while I'm still in this good mood. Why go home and just be in my room by myself, doing nothing? It'll just get depressing again.

She's sitting in her comfy chair and she's asleep, her head tucked against her hand. Aunt Em must've been here this week because fresh flowers are on the table beside Meredith. Pink carnations. She loves pink carnations because they were in her wedding bouquet.

It's hard not to wonder whether she was always glad she married Granddad and had an instant family, or whether she eventually found out about Cynthia Maxwell and realized she was stuck in a no-win situation. But she's got Dad and Aunt Em. And me and Mom. That counts for something.

"Oh," says Meredith, waking up and lifting her head. She looks at me for a couple of seconds. "I didn't expect you today."

I sit close to her and take her hand. "Hi, Meredith. It's Emily."

"Emily."

I can't tell if she knows who I am. Probably not. "When I was on the bus coming here, I was thinking about that time I stayed with you and Granddad and you were doing some housecleaning."

"Oh?" she says, and sits up a bit straighter to listen.

"I was maybe four. I stood on the kitchen counter and wiped off the fronts of all your cupboard doors while you held onto my legs in case I lost my balance. Then you emptied out some other cupboards, ones lower down, and I crawled inside to clean them."

I'm wondering if she's picturing what I'm picturing. "Afterwards we made cookies with candies for faces. You put one of your aprons on me, but it was way too big so you folded it up around my waist. I stood on a chair and you let me add sugar and stuff."

"That was fun," says Meredith, and I know she doesn't actually remember doing all that but she means it sounds like fun the way I'm telling it.

"Yeah," I say.

Her hand is cool against mine, and the rings on her fingers are loose. Tiny bluish veins run like miniature rivers under her pale skin. This is the hand of a person who's known me my entire life. I like how this makes me feel.

She looks down at our hands together and then she looks back up. There's a quiet peacefulness in her eyes, like she's calmly waiting for me to continue. So I tell her about when we went shopping and it was maybe my first time on a bus, and about eating at a food court and how she let me have onion rings. And then I tell her about the Christmas we all had to go to her and Granddad's because the power went off at our place. Mom packed up everything—the half-cooked turkey and all the vegetables peeled and ready for pots. And the mince pies. It was like going on a camping trip. Aunt Em came too, of course. Then all of us stayed overnight, including Aunt Em, even though the power wasn't off at her place.

"That was one of the best Christmases!" I say.

She has a nice big smile, which makes me feel really, really good.

One of the personal care workers comes in. "They're going to sing Christmas carols down in the lounge," she says. "You should take your grandmother. It's the elementary school choir." She goes over and gently wakes Rose to tell her about the Christmas carols.

"Let's go see the elementary school choir!" I say with exaggerated enthusiasm. "This'll put us in the Christmas mood. Only a few weeks to Christmas, you know."

Meredith's not so steady on her feet as I help her up, so I hang onto her arm and reach for her walker.

"That's it. You're doing good," says the care worker. I'm not sure if she's talking to Rose or Meredith or me.

We get to the lounge, where the elementary school choir is starting to line up and their teacher is testing out a few notes on the piano. All the children are wearing white shirts or blouses, and red and green ribbon ties. One boy is wearing one of those antler headbands. Cute.

I find two chairs near the front and help Meredith settle into one of them. Someone is passing around booklets of the Christmas carols, and I say we'll share one. The man next to me is holding his upside down. A few people have already fallen asleep in their wheel-chairs. The care workers are standing close by. *Like shepherds keeping watch by night.*

The children begin to sing and Meredith studies the whole scene, tapping her hand against her leg. After the first song, they tell us all to join in. "Away in a Manger." Everyone knows that. I hold the page up for Meredith but she just watches the children. I sing along, listening to those tiny kid voices mixed in with the frail, whispery old voices. Meredith bows her head when everyone sings, *"The little Lord Jesus..."*

On my way home on the bus, I think about Meredith. How she was asleep when I got there and how she listened so carefully when I talked about cleaning cupboards and making cookies with faces and eating onion rings at a food court and having family Christmas sleepovers. I'm glad I was there to sit with her while everyone sang carols.

"You're late getting home from school," says Dad, letting the newspaper crinkle down to the floor beside his chair.

"Actually," I say, "I went to see Meredith."

"Oh? Any special reason?"

"Just felt like it, I guess. I yakked away about all kinds of stuff we used to do when I was little."

Dad's face gets all dreamy, like he's pushing away the recently revealed history of our family and trying to remember some of those fun times too. "She'd like that, in her own way."

"And then we went to hear a kids' choir sing Christmas carols. Seems a bit early for carols, though."

"Old people don't care if it's early or late," says Dad. "They'd still enjoy the familiar songs and the memories."

"Remember that Christmas the power went out?"

Mom hears me as she comes into the living room. "I sure do. At least we had somewhere to go and cook our Christmas dinner."

"And we all stayed the night," says Dad. "I don't

think the power came back on over here till the next morning."

"Oh, the lumps in that old hide-a-bed," says Mom.

"You made French toast for breakfast, Dad. I remember that. And Aunt Em went next door to get maple syrup because Granddad and Meredith didn't have any. Then you and Granddad came back here to check on stuff, but me and Mom stayed with Meredith."

"We did?"

"Just till the furnace got going."

"Oh, yes. I remember now."

We're picturing that Christmas like it happened yesterday, which puts us all in the same kind of easygoing mood.

As I'm setting the table for dinner, I decide I'll go see Meredith every once in a while and tell her about some happy times I remember that she doesn't remember anymore.

Ten

Before Leo even says anything, I know something's wrong.

Everyone's pushing past us in the hall. He steps closer to the wall and I do too.

"Mom flunked rehab." He tries to smile, but it fades fast. "She signed herself out, then went to a motel and drank herself stupid. Now they won't let her back in rehab. At least, not the same place."

"What'll she do?"

"Who knows?" He looks over his shoulder at people passing by, but I know he's not really paying attention to what he's seeing. "She's back home."

That explains why he wasn't on the bus this morning. Same old scenario.

So I say, "Does Caroline know?"

"Not yet. I'm going to Jane's tomorrow to stay for

the weekend. If Mom's sober, she'll come with me."

I'm not ready for how his eyes look. "I'm sorry, Leo."

We just stand there.

"I'm really sorry."

"I know," he says.

I don't realize what I'm doing until I touch his hand and then I hold his fingers. They're large and rough and cold. I can feel the cold of his fingers seeping into my hand.

It was scary hitchhiking without Leo. But ever since I woke up this morning, I've been thinking about him. About having a chance to talk and find out if things are working out okay. So I hitchhiked to North West Cove.

Jane answers the door and she's surprised to see me. "Emily! Come in! How'd you get here?"

I hold up my thumb and smile.

"Don't tell me you hitchhiked! All by yourself? Emily, that's so dangerous!"

"It was okay."

She closes the door and we go into the kitchen. "Leo. Emily's here."

I can't tell what he's thinking. Boy, does he look tired.

"You hitchhike?"

"Yeah."

"Take long?"

"Not really. Got a ride to exit five then another one almost right away to exit six. Took a while to get down here, though."

"A very dangerous thing," says Jane. "She's picking up your bad habits, Leo."

"My bad habits? I never hitchhike alone." Now he's almost smiling. "I always have a female with me."

"Oh, you!" she says and smacks him on the arm. "Make your guest some cocoa to warm her up." Before she leaves the kitchen, she turns and says, "You won't be hitchhiking home. When Dan gets back with Caroline, he'll drive you."

No one's mentioned Leo's mother.

Leo makes cocoa and I want to ask a ton of questions, but I don't.

He puts the mugs on the kitchen table and we sit down. "Looks like I'm changing schools again," he says.

This just about knocks me over. "How come?"

"It's a long story."

"Meaning it's none of my business."

He takes a deep breath. "Mom's going to another rehab. In Toronto. We can't keep the apartment."

"So you'll live here?"

"For a while."

"Mom leaves tomorrow morning. After that, I'll head back to the city and start packing things up."

"Is your mother home now?"

"Yeah. A friend of hers is with her to make sure she stays sober."

"Maybe it'll be different this time," I say.

His face changes. It's harder. Colder. "No, it won't. It'll be just like the last time and all the other times before that. It's fucking hopeless!"

"Leo." Jane is standing in the doorway.

He looks at her, gets up, grabs his jacket, and leaves. He doesn't slam the door.

"I'm sorry, Emily. Leo's so—"

"I know."

"You came all this way."

"It's okay."

"Did he tell you about moving here?"

"Yeah. At least he'll be with Caroline."

Jane smiles but not in a happy way.

"Maybe I'll go find him," I say. "He's probably not far."

"Don't you hitchhike back to the city, Emily. Please."

"I won't. I promise."

I can see Leo standing by himself down on the wharf. He's not going to like me coming after him like this. Maybe I should just head for the highway and break my promise to Jane. But I have a plan and I want to do it before I think about it too much, so I keep on walking.

"Here."

He ignores me.

"Take this, Leo."

He still ignores me but I know he sees the rock in my hand. His anger rock. It's been in my pocket ever since he gave it to me. I'm not leaving. I can be just as stubborn as him. I'll stand here holding this rock till my hand freezes off.

Finally he says, "What's that for?" He still doesn't look at me.

"I want you to take it and throw it out in the water as far as you can."

"What'll that prove?"

"That you don't have to be angry."

For a couple of seconds he doesn't move, but then he slowly takes the rock from my hand and holds it in his fist.

I look out past the end of the wharf, past the old rowboat that's tied there, and past the waves rolling in. I wait for the rock to fly up in the air and then disappear with a splash. But nothing happens.

I turn around in time to see Leo walk away.

"I'm only trying to help!"

He keeps walking.

SYLVIA GUNNERY

I look around for his anger rock but I can't find it.

A car comes down the hill and stops beside Leo for a second. Then it keeps coming out to the wharf. It's Dan. I recognize him from that picture with Jane.

"Hi," I say. "Sorry to make you drive all the way to the city."

"No problem. Good chance to pick up a few things we can't get out here in the boonies. Jane gave me a list," he says with a grin.

I like how he doesn't ask about why Leo was walking up the hill while I was still back on the wharf. And he doesn't bring up the topic of Leo's mother or the Toronto rehab. After we gab for a few minutes about how cold it is, we mostly listen to the radio and don't say much.

My cell beeps and I take it out of my pocket. It's a text from Jenn about a party at her place tonight. I'm totally not expecting this.

"Always connected," says Dan. "Not that that's a bad thing, I suppose. But I'm sure glad my folks couldn't track me down when I was a teenager." He looks over at me and laughs. "That would've been a disaster."

"It's about a party tonight at my friend's." I think about saying former friend, but I don't. Too complicated.

"Oh, that's different. A party. Good to know about a party."

144

We go back to listening to music on the radio. I'm thinking about Jenn's message, and then it hits me. She likely just texted everyone on her friends list. Even former friends she hasn't deleted from her list yet.

And, for some weird reason, I decide I'll go to Jenn's party.

The place is packed, and for a while I don't even see Jenn. Everyone's here.

Ever since I got Jenn's text, I've been picturing Brian at this party. He's on her list too, or at least he used to be. I'm not saying I'm not nervous about seeing him because I am. And by now he must have the Xmas card. That doesn't bother me, though. I meant every sarcastic sentiment.

I put my jacket on top of the pile of coats and jackets on the floor of Jenn's Mom's "study," as she calls it. I walk past the living room where music's blasting and everyone's dancing. I go into the crowded kitchen and see Jenn and Ronny shaking chips into a large bowl and spooning salsa into a smaller bowl. They look like they're having fun. He's putting a salsa-smeared chip into her mouth when she finally sees me.

"M-mily!" she says through the mouthful.

No way was she expecting to see me here.

She chews and swallows in an exaggerated way, trying not to laugh because now Ronny's mocking her by making his cheeks puff out like a chipmunk's.

It starts to feel like it used to be with me and Jenn, laughing our heads off in this kitchen about something really lame. Well, not exactly like it used to be, with all these people here. But anyway, I relax a little. So far, no Brian.

"You by yourself?"

"Yeah." I get that she means *by yourself* as in *without Leo*, but I avoid that topic. "Great party! Everyone's here."

Ronny takes the bowls of chips and salsa into the living room.

Then Jenn says, "Did you see Brian? He's here somewhere."

My stomach turns upside down and I feel panic crawl up into my throat. I can't believe this. My face feels blood red.

"Emily! You're blushing!"

So now, practically everyone in this kitchen is checking out that I'm blushing and, surprise, I blush even more.

"Come on, Emily. This is crazy. Let's go find Brian. It's not like you can't talk to the guy. Who knows, maybe he's changed his mind and—"

"Jenn!" I say, and it comes out sounding like I'm shouting at a little kid who's about to put a finger in a light socket. I calm my voice down and hope only she can hear me. "Brian has not changed his mind." I say this very carefully. "But I have."

Ronny comes back to the kitchen, grabs Jenn's hand, and takes her to the living room to dance. She looks over her shoulder in a kind of puzzled way for a split second, then turns and bounces along after Ronnie in time to the music. It makes me smile.

I get my coat from off the pile and head out the front door without looking back. As I walk along the street, I start singing the song that's blasting out from the house. It makes me think of what Leo said that night we were practicing for our project that didn't happen. He was right. If I don't get all self-conscious thinking about my voice, it doesn't sound too bad.

I sleep in way late so no one's home when I finally get up. Mom and Dad are visiting Meredith as usual because it's Sunday morning.

I'm making toast when the back door opens and Aunt Em comes in.

"Hi." I take the jam out of the fridge. "Mom and Dad are visiting Meredith."

"Yes," she says. "I just saw them. They arrived as I was leaving." She's smiling, but it's an odd smile. Sort of heavy.

"Is everything okay?"

"I need you to know something, Emily. Come and sit down."

We sit at the table and she picks up my hand. I think of holding Meredith's hand.

A small, panicky feeling starts creeping in.

"When Dana and Myra were here, I told you that your mom lost her baby. How he was stillborn."

Her eyes are so serious I can't look away.

"When our mother died, Gerry and I were much too young to grasp what was happening. But the death of his child…I had never seen Gerry so devastated. And then the doctors told Winnie she should never risk another pregnancy."

"But—"

"I decided I would have a baby for them."

"What?"

"When you were only minutes old, Winnie held you and Gerry gave you your name."

"What are you talking about?" I pull my hand away and stand up. "This is stupid!"

"It isn't stupid," she says quietly. "It's the truth." She stands up and puts her hand on my arm.

"Don't touch me!"

"Emily."

"If you're supposed to be my mother, then who's supposed to be my father?" I'm almost not breathing.

She looks right into my eyes but she doesn't answer.

I feel like I'm falling off a cliff.

"I went to a clinic."

I can't stand how afraid I feel right now. I can't move.

"Look at me, Emily."

I can't.

"Please."

My heart's pounding and pounding and my stomach's squeezed tight.

"Look at me. I need to know you're okay."

"I'm not okay!" I'm screaming but I can't help it. "How can I be okay? Mom's not Mom? You're not Aunt Em? And Dad's not my real father? This is crazy!" I can hardly think.

"You need to know the truth."

"Well I don't care about the truth!"

I run upstairs and she doesn't follow me. I'm taking deep, deep breaths and forcing myself not to cry. If I cry I'll go insane.

Nothing she said makes sense. Nothing. Maybe it's a

lie. Is she crazy? Maybe she's crazy.

I try to calm myself and wait for Mom and Dad to get home. If something's wrong with Aunt Em, they'll help. Something must be wrong.

When I hear Dad's car, I run downstairs. Aunt Em is sitting at the kitchen table as Dad comes in. Mom's behind him.

For a second, we're all frozen in place.

"What's the matter?" Mom looks at me and then at Aunt Em. "I want you to tell me what's the matter," she says.

"She said you're not my mother!"

But I already know the truth from the look on Mom's face.

Eleven

"Why?" Mom hasn't moved.

"It wasn't right that she didn't know."

"We're her parents, Emma. It was up to us whether to tell her. It was not up to you! Behind our backs!"

"Wait," says Dad. "Wait. Let's keep calm."

"Emily," says Mom softly.

I don't know what to do.

"Here, Winnie. Give me your coat," says Dad. "Sit down. Everyone sit down."

Mom comes over and holds me. I close my eyes and try to breathe.

"Please," says Dad, "let's all just sit down together and talk this through."

"When we adopted Emily, there was absolutely no mention of ever telling her." Mom's voice sounds so tight.

151

"Or of not telling her."

When we adopted Emily. I can't breathe.

"Hold on," says Dad very patiently. "I said we need to talk. Not argue. In my mind, it's Emily we should be listening to right now."

We sit together at the kitchen table like we've done a hundred thousand times before.

They all look at me.

"Nothing's the same," I say. "It's too confusing. I'm scared."

"There's nothing for you to be afraid of," Dad says.

"She told me she went to a clinic."

"Oh, God," says Mom.

"Let her talk," says Dad. "Please."

"So no one actually knows who my father is." I don't look at Dad right now.

"That isn't true," says Aunt Em. "We know a lot about your father. The screening is very thorough. It is not a casual process. You'll be able to learn as much about him as we know."

"Like what?"

"What he likes to do in his spare time. His hair color. His eyes. What he studied at university. Lots of things."

"But not his name," I say.

Mom stands up. "I want you to leave our house, Emma."

"Winnie—"

"I mean it, Gerry. We need to be alone now. As a family."

"Emma is part of this family," says Dad.

"After what she's done to Emily? To us? No."

"It's okay, Gerry. I'll go."

"That won't solve anything."

"It'll give everyone time to think."

"Think?" Mom's really mad now. She says, "How much thinking did you do before you came here and upset Emily, telling her things she didn't need to know!"

"She did need to know, Winnie. What were we going to do? Keep up a façade until some stranger comes along after we're dead and tells her that what she thought was true all her life isn't? Is that what you want for her?"

The kitchen gets suddenly quiet. I know we're all thinking about Granddad. And Cynthia Maxwell and Dana.

Tears start running down Mom's face and Dad gets up and puts his arms around her.

"I'm sorry, Winnie," says Aunt Em. "I couldn't let that happen to my daughter." She looks at me. "It would hurt you too much, Emily. Even more than it may be hurting you now. At least you still have us to help you understand."

When we hear the front door shut, Mom comes over and holds me in a very tight hug. I feel her tears on my forehead. This makes me even more afraid. I won't let myself cry. I take a deep breath and hold it for a few seconds before I let it out without making a sound. I know Mom can feel my breath move through my body. She doesn't say anything, but I can feel her head turn toward Dad. I know the hurt look that's on her face, even though I can't see it.

Then I say, "I'm going upstairs."

"Emily—"

"I'm not even dressed yet," I say, like a kind of excuse.

When I'm in the shower, I just stand there for a long time, letting water run down my face.

On the way back to my room, I hear the sound of Mom and Dad talking in their bedroom. The door's closed, so I can't hear what they're saying. Most of it's Mom's voice, but here and there Dad says a few quiet words.

Mom and Dad.

I'm sitting on my bed, brushing and brushing my hair, when I hear Dad outside my door. "Emily."

The door opens.

"Mind if I come in?"

I shrug my shoulders because I know I'm going to cry. Dad. My Dad. My perfect and calm and wonderful Dad.

"Don't cry, Emily. There's no reason for those tears."

"Everything's changed."

"I'm still Dad. Mom's still Mom. That's the way it's always been and that's the way it always will be." He sits beside me, his shoulders slumped and his eyes trying to fake not being sad.

He's got papers in his hand.

"I want you to see these, Emily. These are your adoption papers. And this is an agreement all of us signed not long after Emma told us you were on the way. You need to know without any doubt whatsoever that we agreed to be your family before you were even born. And we've loved you since before you were born. I don't want you to be confused or afraid."

I look down at the papers but I don't pick them up.

"Where's Mom?"

"She's resting."

"Will she be mad if I see these?"

"No. We've talked about it."

"I don't know if I want to see them."

"Then I'll leave them here. You can decide later." He gets up, puts the papers on my desk, and leaves.

When I go downstairs, Mom's still in their bedroom and I can hear Dad out in his shed, sawing something. I know it's not fair, but I leave the house without saying anything to them.

The air smells like rain. I stuff my hands in my pockets and then I think about Leo's anger rock because it's not in my pocket anymore.

I can't get my head around everything.

In my mind I can see all of us this morning. Mom crying. She never cries. Dad with that look when he gave me the adoption papers.

I can picture us a zillion years ago when things were normal. Mom's putting maybe macaroni and cheese on everyone's plate, and she's smiling at Dad and Aunt Em because they're laughing about something.

And it's in the same kitchen where we were today, with Mom telling Aunt Em to leave and Dad saying she's part of our family. And Aunt Em saying, "My daughter."

Aunt Em. It's like she doesn't exist anymore.

What I don't get is if they all talked about the adoption and signed those papers, then why didn't they figure out that I wouldn't be a baby forever and someday I'd somehow find out? They should've told me when I was maybe six or seven. What would've been wrong with that? Little kids get used to whatever they need to get used to because everything in life is new. It's no big deal. Not like being seventeen. It makes me mad.

The more I think about this, the madder I get.

And how much did Granddad know, anyway? He'd have to be blind not to see his own daughter was pregnant. I can picture the expression on his face when the obvious became obvious. As if he had any right to be self-righteous. Now that I think of it, all this probably explains why he never much liked being a grandfather. I'd be this constant reminder of all the brutal details.

I turn up Leo's street and head toward his apartment building. I go in and ring the buzzer, hoping he's back from Jane's by now.

"Yeah?" It's Leo's voice.

"It's Emily," I say.

He doesn't say anything.

I'm thinking I should go.

Then I see him walking down the stairs. He opens the door. "What's up with this?" *This* meaning me, interfering in his life and showing up when I'm not invited.

I start to cry and I know Leo won't get why I'm crying, but I can't stop. "This has nothing to do with you," I manage to say.

"Good," he says. Then he sighs this big sigh. "Look, I need to get the packing done."

I picture bureau drawers open and boxes on the floor. I wipe my eyes. "You shouldn't have to do all that packing by yourself."

"Jane and Dan are coming later."

"Can I come in for a minute?" Then I say, "I need to use the bathroom."

He looks at me like he doesn't believe me.

"Really," I say.

"Okay."

I pour cold water into the bathroom sink and splash my eyes. They're still red but I can't do anything about that. I look around. There's a little toothbrush with a zebra head. Caroline's. There's an electric razor and a blow dryer plugged in. For some odd reason there's a guitar pick stuck in a hairbrush. And there's face cream and earrings and hairspray and a miniature jade bird and perfume and a plant that needs to be watered and soap shaped like roses that no one's used.

I go into the kitchen where Leo's emptying out a cupboard. "I could pack up what's in the bathroom. I won't get in your way."

He looks like he doesn't have enough energy to even stand there.

"Just for half an hour," I say. "Here. I'll take these two boxes and fill them."

"Wait." He picks up a garbage bag and says, "Some stuff should go in here."

Towels and facecloths and sheets and pillowcases from a narrow closet next to the bathtub almost fill the two boxes. A lot of stuff by the sink and in the cupboard underneath I just dump in the garbage bag. But I carefully wrap the jade bird in some tissue and tuck it in with the towels.

Then I water the plant.

"Okay," I say. "Bathroom's finished."

"Thanks." Leo looks amazingly tired.

My stomach's hurting from being so empty. There's a box of crackers on the counter so I reach in and grab a few. They're a bit stale. "Guess my half-hour's up," I say.

Leo's wrapping knives and forks in newspaper and putting them into a box.

"Or I could keep packing stuff."

He doesn't look at me. "Sure. Okay."

"Where?"

"How about Caroline's room?"

I pick up more boxes. "What if I write on these? You know, clothes, toys, books…"

"Yeah."

It's way easier packing up Caroline's room because I can picture her unpacking and feeling pretty happy to see her stuff again.

I'm dragging the box of toys out to the hallway when I realize that Leo's standing there, leaning against the wall. He's crying. Just letting tears slide down his face and fall on the front of his sweater. Across from him, the door of his mother's bedroom is open.

"When Jane comes, she'll pack everything in there," I say. I get some tissue from the bathroom and give it to him.

He wipes his eyes and face but tears just keep on coming.

I don't know what to say. I lean against the wall beside him and close my eyes. He's making small swallowing sounds and very quiet sniffing sounds. All this gives me a real helpless feeling. Deep and sad and helpless.

After a few minutes, he walks back toward the kitchen. I follow him.

He pours a glass of water and drinks it without turning around. "I threw that rock away."

"You did?"

"I was waiting for a ride in the middle of nowhere and I took it out of my pocket and threw it in the woods as far as I could. I heard it crack into a tree."

"And now you're not mad?"

"Being mad's useless. It won't change anything." He picks up a box, opens another drawer, and starts packing again.

"I'm glad you threw it away," I say.

"Yeah."

I watch him put a cheese grater and a can opener and a frying pan into the box. I'm wondering where he'll be when these boxes get unpacked. I'm wondering if his mother'll be there with him and Caroline. "I probably should go."

"Yeah."

"Want me to take any garbage bags out?"

"Sure. Okay. There's a bin around back."

I get the bag from the bathroom and pick up another one beside the kitchen door. They're stuffed but not real heavy.

"Thanks."

"No problem." I start clunking down the stairs. Then it hits me. "You won't be going to school tomorrow."

"Not till after Christmas."

"But I mean, you won't be at our school anymore." *You won't be on the bus. You won't be in class. You won't be around the next time Brian shows up, and what if I panic all over again? And what about Sam?* "Will you still be seeing Sam?"

"Sure. I'm not moving to Mars."

"Right." I clunk the rest of the way down the steps.

"See ya," he says.

"See ya."

When I get to the garbage bin, I notice a box of empty bottles next to it. Not that they have to be Leo's mother's, but that's what I'm thinking as I heave the bags into the bin.

Dad's looking out the front door when I get home. "Stopped raining, did it?" he says as I step inside. I know he's trying to make me think he was just looking out to check the weather.

"Pretty much," I say.

Then he asks, "How are you doing now?"

"I'm not sure."

"Well," he gives a small sigh, "go in the kitchen and see your mother. She tried to call you. She's been worried."

The kitchen smells good, a mix of something spicy and the musty smell of baked potatoes.

Mom stops drying a bowl. "I tried to call you but your cellphone wasn't on. It's hard enough, Emily, without worrying all day about where you were."

I know things haven't turned out the way Mom wanted, but the same goes for me. It's depressing that my life depended on a little baby being stillborn. I can't stand it. "I know you had a stillborn baby."

Mom gives me a look like I just threw something at her and missed. Then she opens the cupboard and puts the bowl away. "Emma, again, no doubt."

"I'm sorry you lost your baby."

Now she's wiping the countertop, lifting the toaster to clean underneath. "It was a long time ago."

"But you must think about him. What he would've been like."

She stops cleaning and looks at me. Everything's quiet for a few seconds. Then she says, "And now I'm losing you."

Twelve

I head to the music room to find out if Sam's around. From the end of the hall I hear music, mostly tuba.

The door's closed but I see Sam through the narrow window, practicing with four or five people. Like everything's normal.

I go back to my locker, shove my books in, and head out through the front doors. I'm thinking about the small jade bird. It doesn't take much to give you the feeling you know someone, even if you never met that person.

"Emily! Hey, Emily! Where're you going?"

Brian's in the parking lot in his mother's car.

"Nowhere." He can probably see I'm starting to panic.

"Need a drive?"

"No."

"Come on, Em. We have to at least talk."

"You have a girlfriend." Panic is sloshing in my stomach and I try to calm it down.

"Look, I said I was sorry. I didn't expect to meet someone so soon."

So soon.

"Maybe we can go get your Christmas tree. Like last year."

"Nothing's like last year, Brian. Nothing." There's no way he has a clue what I'm really talking about, but I don't care.

I cut across the lawn and down to the sidewalk. If Brian follows me, I won't be impressed.

A car slows down and stops. I turn around fast, ready to shout something obscene.

"I thought that was you." Dana's leaning across the passenger seat, looking up at me through the opened window. "Hop in."

Why would Dana be here again? Has something happened on top of everything else? I get into the car and brace myself.

"What gives with leaving school when it's barely nine o'clock?" She says this in a curious way, not in a blaming way.

"Didn't feel like staying." I keep it simple. "So how come you're here?"

"Emma called. She was pretty upset about how things turned out yesterday. I figured she could use some support. And maybe you, too."

"What's that supposed to mean?" My voices gets this whiny-kid sound like I'm picking a fight, when really I don't feel like arguing about anything because right now I don't have the energy.

"How about if we go back to school and get permission for you to leave? Must still be rules against skipping, unless schools've miraculously transformed themselves into bastions of liberalism."

Dana doesn't go into any explanations. She just tells the school secretary she's my aunt and that I won't be attending classes today.

The secretary gives her usual raised-eyebrow look because she'd never in a million years believe anyone had a legitimate reason to leave school, especially so early in the day. She glances at the clock and neatly prints the time on the permission form: 9:12. "Sign here, please."

Dana writes her name in huge loopy letters that sprawl across the bottom of the form. Something else for the secretary to raise her eyebrow about.

"How'd you know what school I go to?"

"Emma. But it wasn't her idea to come here. Her theory is that all of you just need time, and things will work themselves out."

I don't say anything.

"Silence never works."

I'm not sure if she's talking about me. Never means never, I guess. But right now I have absolutely nothing to say.

"Is there a place we can grab a coffee and hang for a while?" She pulls away from the curb and we head downtown. "Later we can meet Emma for lunch."

"Why?"

"To talk."

A small burst of fear leaps into my throat and I suddenly realize what I'm afraid of. Seeing her again. Talking to her.

"There's a coffee place over there. Good. You like coffee? Sure you do. What's not to like? Though Myra's convinced I consume too much caffeine. I won't say she's wrong."

We sit by a window at a small round table with two metal not-so-comfortable chairs. Dana gets a tall mug of black coffee and I order a cappuccino, which I like because of the foamy milk.

"A lot of information's coming at you all at once," she says. "Pretty tough stuff to handle."

I concentrate on the cinnamon speckles on top of the cappuccino.

"Maybe if I found out about my birth father when I

was seventeen, it would've been different. It's easier at my age. Mom has her life and I've got mine. She thought she was doing the right thing by keeping her secrets. Just like Emma and your Mom and Dad."

I don't say anything but I'm thinking, what's this got to do with her when she doesn't know any of us anyway?

"Are you determined not to speak, Emily? I'm just trying to help."

"You don't actually know any of us, so what makes you think you can help?"

"Ouch. Not that I don't deserve that, if it's how you feel."

She sips her coffee and looks out at traffic for a couple seconds, while I think about getting up and walking out of here.

"The way I see it," she says, "is you can dig yourself into a hole when stuff happens or you can find ways to deal with it. When Mom was forced to tell me that Dad wasn't my birth father, it was a shock. Big time. Then I find out about Emma and Gerry and the potential for a whole extended family, including a niece." She gives me this big smile. "Too cool."

No way I'm in the mood to smile back. "What about how your mother cheated on your father and lied about it for so long? How cool was that?"

She looks into her coffee cup like it's empty, but then she takes a sip. She knows I'm trying on purpose to hurt her. I'm not saying I don't feel bad about what I'm doing. "My life's not your life."

"I'm not implying that."

"At least you know who your real father was."

"Real. Hm." She gives this bent little smile. "Dad believed he was my dad, and I believed he was my dad. We loved each other right up to the day he died. I still love him. Doesn't get more real than that. And, of course, it's too late to meet Karl."

Her eyes are this mix of green and brown. Serene. It makes me look away.

"They all love you, Emily. Gerry. Emma. Winnie. I don't think one of them loves you more or less than the others. That love's been there at the center of their lives since the day you were born."

I think of Dad holding the adoption papers and the agreement papers. *Before you were even born.*

She looks at her watch. "I'll call Emma and see when she's free for lunch. You coming with us?"

"No."

"I'll drive you home, then."

When I get out of the car, she doesn't say anything and neither do I.

Mom asks me why I'm home from school and I fake

being sick, even though she knows I'm faking. Soon she'll find out Dana's back, if she doesn't know already.

"Dana is staying over at Emma's." Dad says this to Mom but he's looking at me, because if he knows Dana's here, he knows I saw her today.

"She didn't need to be brought into this." Mom lifts the cover off the potatoes like they need to be checked. She's got this stubborn look on her face that tells Dad there's no use talking right now.

He scratches his head, then lets his hand fall to his side, watching Mom clatter the top back on the pot. The way he looks and the way she looks and the clanking sound of that pot cover is all very depressing. It feels like we'll be like this forever.

The kitchen phone rings and makes me jump.

"It's for you," says Dad. "It's your friend, Leo."

"Leo?" I take the phone and walk into the living room.

"Leo?"

"Yeah."

"How come you're calling?"

"Wondering how things are."

"With me?"

"Yeah."

I know he's talking about me crying yesterday. I just say, "I'm okay."

"Caroline was real happy about getting the junk you packed."

"Good. I'm glad."

"Any interesting crap at school?"

"Didn't stay long enough to find out." Right away I wish I hadn't said that. "I saw Sam practicing with the tuba guy and a couple others."

"What's up with not staying at school?"

"Just didn't feel like it."

"Oh."

There he goes again. Minding his own business, which is one of the reasons I like him so much. "I saw Brian in the parking lot when I was leaving. He said we should talk. Maybe get a Christmas tree like we did last year."

"And?"

"I told him it's not the same as last year."

"Smart."

"Yeah."

"So, anyway, Jane's getting supper. I should go."

"Leo?"

"What?"

"I know you're sort of wondering about why I was crying yesterday, and in a way I want to talk about it, but I just can't right now. It's complicated."

"Right." He waits a couple of seconds and then says, "Crap usually is."

Dad's setting the table so I get some glasses and put them on the placemats. Then I pour milk in two glasses and water in Dad's.

When we're having dinner, I decide to try a conversation to smooth things out a bit. I tell them about Leo's mother going to rehab in Toronto and about how Leo and Caroline have to live with Jane in North West Cove.

"It will be a while before that little girl truly understands what's happening," says Dad. "She's too young right now."

"Kids figure stuff out. And they can handle more than adults give them credit for." I don't try to keep the sharp edge off what I'm saying.

Dad looks at Mom and she looks down at her plate. It feels like we're all stuck in quicksand.

If you ever get stuck in quicksand, you're supposed to lie flat so you spread out your weight and you won't sink like a stone into the guck. I remember learning about that in elementary school. But are you just supposed to lie there? Shouldn't you edge your way along, very cautiously, until you reach solid ground? Because if you just lie there, you'd eventually sink. Maybe more slowly, but you'd still sink. I'm sure of that.

Dad says, "Sooner or later, we're going to have to

invite Emma back into our home." He doesn't sound frustrated or tired or depressed. Just telling it like it is.

"I need time," says Mom.

"This involves more people than only you," he says carefully. "Dana has made a special trip down here, and before she goes back, I think we need to bring the family together and get on with our lives."

"Sounds simple," says Mom, but she doesn't mean it.

"We at least have to try." Dad looks at me.

I get up from the table and take my dishes over to the sink.

"I'll do those," says Mom. "You have homework."

That's what she always says, because to Mom, homework's like the biggest deal. Sacred. All my life I've used homework as an excuse to get out of doing what I didn't want to do. Right now, this makes me feel immensely sad. I wish I could tell her I'm sorry about taking advantage of her like that. I wish I could tell her I realize how weird she feels, now that I know she's not my actual mother. But all I say is, "I'll do the dishes. There's not much homework so close to Christmas."

"I want Dana and Emma to come here for dinner tomorrow night," says Dad.

Mom and I pull ourselves back from the distraction of dishes.

"I know it'll be awkward," he says. "But we have to start somewhere."

"I'm in no mood to cook a meal for—"

"Then we'll order in. Chinese. We haven't done that in a long time." Dad's smiling but it's not contagious.

I start rinsing plates and stacking them in the dishwasher. Mom plugs in the kettle. We're both not saying anything. I'm thinking about the look on her face last night when she said, "Now I'm losing you."

"I'm asking you both to give this a try. Please."

"What if they don't want to come?"

But Dad's ahead of me. "I already asked them and they said yes."

Mom's not expecting this. "What?"

"If Emily or you absolutely don't want this dinner to happen, it won't happen. That's what we agreed. All I'm saying is there's no sense in prolonging what's inevitable. We're not going to become a family split into factions. That's never been our style and it's not going to become our style."

I already know what Mom's decision will end up being. Look at the gazillion times Granddad was invited when she didn't really want him here.

Dad looks at me. "Emily?"

"It won't prove anything."

* * *

The papers are on my desk where Dad left them. I wish they weren't here in my room. I wish they didn't exist. I wish none of this ever happened and no one had to sign any adoption papers. I think about taking them downstairs and leaving them on the coffee table just to get them out of here.

I lie down and try to think about nothing. I hate how it gets dark so early now. All the light sucked out of the day. Mega depressing.

I close my eyes and picture summer when the sun shines in here way past dinner time, making a bright line across my bed. And being a little kid, trying to get to sleep when it's still broad daylight and somewhere not far away you can hear older kids playing baseball or street hockey. I almost can get that same peaceful little-kid feeling.

Thirteen

"There's somewhere we need to go, Emily. I've called the school to say you won't be there this morning."

Because of how Mom looks, I know this is about something serious.

"Where're we going?"

She ignores my question and says, "Have some breakfast, then get yourself ready."

When I come downstairs, Mom's wearing her coat and wool hat and she's putting on gloves. "It's cold, so dress warmly," she says.

I get my long knitted scarf from the top shelf and wind it around my neck twice. Then I grab my gloves and cram them into my jacket pockets.

"What about a wool hat?"

"I can put this scarf over my head if I need to."

On the bus, Mom sits by the window and looks out.

For a while, we don't say anything.

I'm extremely curious about where we're going. She said we *need* to go to this place. Not *want*. *Need*. Why *need*? No sense even asking. I'll know real soon.

I try for a bit of conversation and point to a ginger cat curled up in a bookstore window. "Look, Mom. In the window."

She says, "Snoozing."

"We should get a cat."

"And who'd look after it when you're at university?"

"I'd come home a lot."

"You say that now, but…"

The bus goes downtown, along the harbor, up past the library, and along Spring Garden Road.

Mom reaches up and pulls the cord to ring the bell. We get off near the main gate of the Public Gardens. We can't be going there because it's closed for winter.

It's cold and gray and windy, so I put my gloves on and tuck my chin into my scarf. We walk along beside the iron fence that surrounds the Gardens. Two people are feeding ducks through the fence right beside a sign that says, "Please do not feed the ducks."

We stop at the corner and wait for a car to make the turn, and then we cross the street. Now I'm thinking we're going to the hospital because it's only half a block away. But why would we need to go there?

Mom's a few steps ahead of me and I almost stop walking when she turns into the cemetery.

"Where're we going, Mom? At least give me a hint."

"It's just over here," she says.

In this cemetery, the trees are a hundred years old. Maybe more. They're huge, with gigantic trunks and long, empty branches reaching high above us. Some of the tombstones are ancient. A few are leaning sideways or backwards.

Mom turns off the main path and walks along between the rows of headstones. I feel solemn, walking behind her over these graves.

She stops beside a wide black headstone with small clumps of what used to be marigolds in front of it. Dad loves marigolds. He plants them every year by our front doorstep and along the edges of his garden.

I read the names on the headstone. *John Clifford Scott. Rhoda Mary Scott*

"This is your mother and father," I say.

The dates of when they died are less than a year apart, and I remember how Mom always said that after her father passed away, her mother died of a broken heart. Near the bottom of the headstone there's something written in small letters. I step closer.

Grandson. Son of Winifred and Gerald Sinclair.

"He didn't live to have a name," Mom says quietly.

Their stillborn baby.

"He isn't buried here. We didn't even get to see him. But I wanted at least some way to mark his place in this world." She uses a tissue to clear away splashes of dirt from the words. Then she straightens back up, still looking at the headstone. "I knew something was wrong when I couldn't feel the baby pushing. The doctors knew too."

I just stand here. I don't know what to say.

"I always planned to tell you everything when you were old enough to understand. And here you are, a young woman already. Time got away from me."

Young woman. I feel like a kid.

"When we lost our baby, it was the end of everything. I hardly got out of bed. What was there to look forward to. And then Emma tells us what she'd done. So Gerry and I could have a family."

"But she didn't even ask you if you wanted a baby."

"She knew if she told us we wouldn't go along with such a plan."

"So then you really didn't want a baby?" My stomach's all churned up.

"Of course we wanted a baby." Mom's eyes are soft and immensely sad. I'm afraid of how I can see so deep into her feelings.

I get off the bus near school and give a little wave to

Mom from the sidewalk. She looks out and gives me a small smile as the bus pulls away. It's like whatever we do right now has to be in tiny little motions because of how everything's so fragile.

I know I'm not actually going to school today. And I'm definitely not showing up for dinner.

After walking for about a half-hour, I'm freezing cold. So I cross the street and go into a coffee shop to warm up. Hardly anyone's in here right now, just a couple of women sitting together by the window and a guy reading the newspaper in a booth near the back.

I get a cappuccino and sit in one of the booths. The heat from the mug feels really good on my hands.

A guy opens the door and walks in. Out of nowhere I get this instant, crazy reaction. All heat and pins and needles.

I can't stop looking at him. Taking off his gloves. Walking over to the counter. Ordering. Checking his watch. Getting money out of his jacket pocket. Paying. Putting change in the paper cup by the cash register. Picking up his coffee and doughnut.

He goes to a table and puts his stuff down. His nose is very red. And his ears.

I watch his black wool jacket with the collar up and

his red scarf and his jeans. I watch him sit down. I watch him not take off his jacket. I watch him have a sip of coffee. He's got black hair that's short and thick, with a couple of curls hanging down on his forehead. He's maybe twenty.

All of a sudden he's watching me watching him.

My face blasts red. I can't stand it.

If I look back up right now, I know I'll see him looking at me like I'm some kind of idiot.

And of course I have to look back up.

He smiles.

I try to pretend I wasn't actually staring at him and that this is just a normal day and I'm sitting here having a cappuccino in this practically deserted coffee shop and soon I'll have to leave because there's somewhere important I have to go.

He's standing up. Panic. He's coming over here.

"Hey," he says.

I could throw up.

He sits down. "Got your Christmas shopping done?"

My brain's disconnected.

"I'm Jacob."

I can't get myself to say anything. My throat's dry and all I can think about is trying to stop my face from being red. Which makes it even redder.

"You go to Dal?"

"Ah, no," I say.

"That's probably why I haven't seen you in here before."

And then I realize this coffee shop is very close to Dalhousie University, so lots of students likely come here every day. I look around at all the empty tables and booths.

"Place changes during Christmas break," he says, maybe to explain why no students are here now. "So, what's your name?"

"Emily." I'm all of a sudden starting to feel a bit cornered. I look over at the two women by the window. They're not noticing anything that's going on in this booth. Why should they? The guy behind the counter is busy arranging a stack of coffee cans.

"Okay. I get that you're not supposed to talk to strangers. Strangers are mean and evil villains lurking everywhere, waiting to find a beautiful girl—say, sitting in a coffee shop having a cappuccino all by herself—and then they move in for the kill!" He raises both hands toward me and makes them like bear claws while he gives this evil-villain look.

That makes me smile. "It's not that," I say. "I just feel...well, odd." My mind replays *a beautiful girl* a couple of times.

"Why? Because you were checking me out and

then I come over here and sit down with you?" He gives a teasing grin.

I give up on trying not to have a red face.

"Will you do something for me?" he says.

"What?"

"Say: Hi, Jacob! Like you haven't seen me in a long time and you're happy that I'm here."

"Why?"

"Come on. Try it. Just two words. It's an experiment."

So I give in and say, "Hi, Jacob."

"No. Not like that. Surprised and happy."

I say, "Hi, Jacob!" like he asked, and it makes me laugh.

"Hey, Emily! Long time no see! How's things?" He's grinning like we're old friends. Then he says, "There. Now doesn't that make you feel like you know me? It does, doesn't it?"

"You're crazy," I say, but I'm still smiling.

"The experiment's a success!" He leans back and gets comfortable.

After we talk for a few minutes, I start to get comfortable too. I actually end up telling Jacob the story of my life. The whole thing. He's a very good listener. When I tell him about Brian's Xmas card, he laughs out loud. Just like Leo did. Then, when I eventually tell him about being adopted before I was even born, I start to cry.

Jacob reaches over and touches my hand. His fingers are long and soft and warm. "I think what your new aunt said is right. They all love you. It's like you have three parents. How lucky is that?"

I look at the two women by the window, and one of them is glancing over at me. She can see I'm crying.

"Come on," Jacob says. "Let's go get some fresh air."

When we're outside, he gives me a tissue and I blow my nose. A man and woman heading into the coffee shop both look back at me. It's embarrassing, crying out here on the sidewalk where anyone walking by can see me and wonder what's going on.

"My place is about five minutes from here if you want some place to go right now," says Jacob.

His apartment isn't really a whole apartment. It's a very small room where there's kitchen cupboards and a fridge and a stove opposite from where his bed is. There's a sofa and a TV and a coffee table. And books everywhere because he's studying to be a doctor. "Pre-med," he says.

He takes my jacket and scarf and puts them across a chair. I'm not crying now, but that numb kind of sad feeling won't go away.

"Want some tea? Sorry I don't have any coffee." Then he grins and says, "But that's a good thing because running out of coffee is how I got to meet you."

I tell him I don't want anything right now. I sit on the sofa and give a big sigh. I'm still holding the soggy crumpled-up tissue.

The sofa sinks a bit as he sits down beside me. "Feeling better?"

"Mm. A bit. I feel so stupid, crying like that. People staring at me."

"It isn't stupid. You're upset. And who cares what people think, anyway?"

"They probably thought you were splitting up with me." I give a half-smile so he knows I'm trying to be funny.

"No chance of that." He leans in and kisses me.

My body has never felt so intense.

I push my hand against his chest and he stops kissing me.

"I want to wash my face," I say. "It feels all puffy."

I go to the bathroom and close the door. I don't really want to wash my face.

I just stand here. Thinking.

I look in the mirror and then I say out loud to myself, "Emily Sinclair, what are you doing here?"

I don't wait for an answer.

I go back out and stand by the sofa. "Jacob," I say, "don't take this the wrong way, but I shouldn't be here. I'm obviously a basket-case today. My brain's not functioning."

I pick up my jacket and scarf, and I leave.

Jacob follows me out of his apartment and down the hall toward the elevator. "I'm sorry I kissed you, Emily. No. I don't mean that. I loved kissing you. But I shouldn't have kissed you. Not when you're so upset."

"It's okay. Really. I just need to go. It's not complicated."

"Can I call you, Emily? At least give me — "

The elevator doors open and there are two elderly ladies smiling out at us. I step in with them and watch the doors slide across Jacob until he isn't there.

End of story.

There's no way in a million years I'm telling Leo about this.

When I get halfway up our street, I realize there are no lights on in our house. Something's wrong. Even if they canceled out on dinner, Mom and Dad would still be home, wondering where I was. If they tried calling me, my cell's off. I probably shouldn't keep doing that.

I hurry inside.

The message light on the kitchen phone is blinking. "You have one new message. Message one — "

"Emily, it's Dad. I suppose you know your cell-phone's not on. Your mom and I are at the nursing home with Meredith. She had a bit of a fall, but she'll be fine. Let's see...it's almost six now. We shouldn't be too late. I called Emma and Dana to cancel dinner plans. You make yourself something to eat."

There's a pot on the stove with uncooked potatoes chopped up in small squares. A couple of onions are on the cutting board beside a knife. Mom must've been making chowder. I check in the fridge and there's the haddock and scallops.

I pour a glass of milk and eat an apple.

I decide to make the chowder. They might be hungry when they get home. A peace offering. I'm adding the cream when a car comes up our driveway and stops near the back door. Mom and Dad.

But it isn't Mom and Dad.

I turn away from the door. It'd be stupid to take off upstairs so I don't, even though I want to with all my might.

"Emily. We need to talk."

"I don't want to."

"You have no choice. I'm not trying to be unkind, but there are things to face in life and this is one of them. You're not a child."

I can hear her pulling out a chair.

"Come sit down."

I turn around and look at her. I think of saying I don't want to talk about how she's my mother. I already have a mother. But I don't say anything. I sit down.

She pushes an envelope across the table toward me.

It's a small envelope. Creamy colored and plain. There's no name on it.

"I want you to read this, Emily. While I'm here with you."

I feel sort of sick to my stomach about whatever's in this envelope. Like, if there's more stuff I don't know about, I won't be able to stand it. I tear carefully down the side of the envelope and open it. Inside there are three sheets of creamy colored paper, folded once.

My face is burning hot even before I start to read.

To my child,

Today your beginnings have been confirmed. You're on your way. I am going to be a mother. And I'm the happiest I've been for as long as I can remember.

You and I are in this together. Alone and together. For at least a while I can selfishly call you my own.

When it's time, Gerry and Winnie will know. And when you are born, they will be your mom and dad. And I will become your aunt.

All this will no longer be a secret when you finally read my letter.

How strange to be writing to you. The grown-up you. The you who will be confused by the choice I've made. The choices. How will you react? What will you think of me? If you're a boy, or if you're a girl…will it be any different?

Here's what you need to know. I love you intensely. I love you unconditionally. I simply and purely love you.

You won't fully understand, but I need to try to explain. With twins, it's a different world. Twins are to-gether before they even breathe. That togetherness never changes. It's there in a way that probably only twins understand, and it's possible that we don't understand it completely. Gerry and I are separate individuals in lots and lots of ways. But we exist together. We can't help it. We share our lives like it's one life.

If you can grasp even some of this, you will know why I am pregnant now and why, when you are born, you will become Gerry and Winnie's child. Not a replacement for their stillborn baby. Never that. But you will be a great joy in their lives.

And always, always, always in mine.

Somewhere deep inside, a very, very tight feeling grabs me and moves through my whole body. A sob bursts out and I keep sobbing and sobbing. She holds me and rocks me, and says, "I know. I know. Shhhh," over and over again.

It's a long time before I can make myself calm down.

I take the hankie she gives me and I blow my nose.

"It's good to cry," she says.

My eyes are puffed up and I feel numb. I'm making these small whimpering sounds but I can't help it. "Did anyone else read that letter?"

"No one. I sealed it the day I wrote it. It was meant only for you."

"I'm too confused."

"Of course you are."

"I hate this."

"It won't be like this forever."

We're quiet for a few seconds.

Then she says, "Winnie and I had a chance to talk today. I left work and came over when I knew she'd be alone."

I kind of brace myself.

"At first I talked a lot about Gerry and me. She knows how much we love Meredith. She has witnessed that love ever since she met us. I wanted her to think about how it's the same way you feel about her." A big sigh drifts up through her body and then quietly and slowly drifts out.

Everything's too extremely sad sad sad. The little stillborn baby who had no name to put on the head-stone. Me growing secretly inside Dad's twin sister and with no actual father. *Alone and together*.

I lean back and blow my nose. I'm still not looking at her.

She goes to the stove and takes the cover off the chowder. "Winnie said she was making chowder. I didn't think she had time to finish it."

"I made it."

"Let's have some." She gets two bowls out of the cupboard and two spoons.

"Dad gave me the adoption papers."

"He told me." She fills the bowls with chowder.

"I didn't read them."

"Just a bunch of legalese," she says and sort of laughs.

She puts the bowls and spoons on the table.

I pick up the letter, fold it, and tuck it back in the envelope.

She sits down across from me. "Mm. Not bad," she says when she tastes my chowder.

I know we're on thin ice right now. One wrong move and things'll crack all around us. Which makes me think of how I waved that tiny wave at Mom when she was on the bus, and how she smiled that tiny smile back at me. Thin ice. I can hardly stand it.

After she leaves, I go up to my room and put the envelope in my desk. I take the adoption papers downstairs and put them on the coffee table in the living room.

It's not long before car lights come up the driveway and, for sure this time it's Mom and Dad.

"Something smells good in here," says Dad.

"Oh! You made the chowder, Emily!" She gives me this big surprised smile, which makes me feel really good.

"Is Meredith doing okay?"

"She'll be fine after a good night's sleep," says Dad, taking Mom's coat.

"Let's have some chowder, Gerry."

"I'll get it," I say.

Dad takes the coats to the hall closet and Mom starts washing her hands. "Emma was here," she says.

I'm not sure if she says this because of seeing the two bowls in the sink, or if she already knew, anyway.

"Yeah."

"How did that go?"

"I dunno. Okay, I guess."

"Hm."

I can tell she's deciding to leave things alone for now.

Dad comes back to the kitchen and catches onto the cautious atmosphere. Then he puts on a grin and says, "This chowder is just what the doctor ordered."

I sit at the table with them and listen to the exaggerated sounds they make about how perfect my chowder is.

Fourteen

I made a family album. A real one, with everyone being exactly who they are.

Mom gave me two half-filled albums and a shoebox full of photographs. "Take all you want. I meant to organize those myself," she said.

I didn't tell her why I was making this album. It'll be obvious.

When I was almost finished, I realized I needed a picture of Dana and Myra. So I emailed and asked them to send one of when they were in Paris on their honeymoon. At first I didn't ask for a picture of Cynthia Maxwell because it's not like she's family. Then I got thinking about it some more and decided, why not? If she's Dana's mother and Dana's my aunt, then we somehow have to be related, in a tangled-up sort of way.

* * *

I open the album and hold it so Meredith can see.

She leans forward to take a closer look. I fix the pillow behind her so she's more comfortable in her cozy chair. She looks up at me, pauses for a second, and then smiles this little smile.

I know she won't remember anyone in this album, so I start to fill her in.

"This is Rita. She was my grandmother before you. She died in a car accident."

Meredith shakes her head sadly.

"That was a long time ago," I say, in case she's confused and thinks I'm telling her about a car accident that just happened.

"And this is you and Granddad. Karl. It's when you got married. Look at your flowers. Pink carnations. Aren't they beautiful!"

She might not be with me on all this family information, but she's looking at the pictures, so I keep going.

"This one's Dad when he was on a kids' hockey team. I don't think he actually liked playing hockey much. He still watches it on TV, though. And here's Dad and Mom on their honeymoon in Niagara Falls."

"Mm." She runs her finger along the pictures and stops at one of me. It was taken in a photographer's studio. I'm lying on my belly on a table with some kind of velvet over it. I'm starkers. Cute and chubby. Typical baby.

"That's me," I say. "Emma's baby." It's so weird to hear my own voice say that.

"Emma's baby," she says.

"Yes. It's Emily. The baby's name is Emily."

I'm not sure if this confuses her, so I say, "I'm Emily. That's a picture of me when I was a little baby." Then I say, "My mother is Emma." I take a slow breath because of the tense feeling I get.

Then I turn the page. "Here she is. This is Emma. Graduating from law school. She's a lawyer."

"Oh!" Meredith smiles like it's a wonderful surprise.

"And that's you and Granddad and Dad with her. Must've rained that day because Granddad's got his umbrella with him. See?"

The pictures Dana and Myra sent are the last ones in the album.

"Here's Dana and Myra in Paris. They're married. To each other. And they're my aunts. Dad and Emma and Dana are brother and sisters. Half-brother and half-sisters, actually."

I look to see if any of this sinks in. I don't think it does.

The last picture makes me feel all nervous, like if

I'm not careful I could hurt Meredith in a major way. So I softly say, "This is Dana when she was ten years old. That's her dad, Mr. Maxwell, holding the bike so she won't fall. And that's her mother standing beside them. Cynthia."

I decide to just leave it at that. Maybe she knows about Dana and about Cynthia Maxwell. Maybe Grand-dad told her. And maybe he didn't. Maybe, when there's not much you actually remember, some things just don't matter anymore. I don't know.

We look slowly through all the pictures again. I'm pretty sure she's enjoying this. Seeing those faces and hearing me talk about who's who.

"I'll leave this right here beside you, Meredith. It's our family album. We can look at the pictures whenever I visit, okay?"

She watches me move things around on the small table to make room for the album. Then she smiles and says, "There we are."

Which is sort of an ironic thing to say, even though she didn't mean it that way.

I haven't talked to Leo since Monday. But I can't help thinking about him and Caroline. How everything sad gets magnified by Christmas.

Mom and Dad and Emma are using Christmas

as an excuse to avoid talking about what's been happening, and I'm definitely fine with that. It's actually a relief to be preoccupied with lights and ornaments and rearranging the living room to make space for the Christmas tree in front of the window.

We're decorating our tree tonight like we always do, exactly one week before Christmas Day.

The tree stand's not in the garage where it should've been. Dad and I look everywhere for it. The garden shed. The attic. The basement. How could anyone misplace something that huge and metal and bright red?

Finally Dad remembers that the water leaked out of the tree stand last year and he had to throw it away. We'd still have it if Dad could've fixed it. He's happy when he's fixing something. Doesn't matter that it'd be simpler to just go out and buy a new whatever. He heads to the hardware store like a kid going for candy, and comes back with something you'd never think would fix whatever he's fixing. But it always does.

So we have to get a new tree stand. People turn totally into nutcases this close to Christmas. Buying and buying like their lives depended on it. There are long lineups everywhere. Parents are shopping, with gigantic toys and little kids all stuffed together in their shopping carts, and I'm wondering how they can do that without the kids figuring out on Christmas morning where their toys came from.

We go to three places and look at two hundred tree stands before Dad finally figures out which one to buy. I don't ask what the magic formula is.

Mom and Emma are taking out the ornaments and organizing them on the sofa. Their usual job. The strings of lights have already been tested and they're in tidy clumps on the floor. We put the stand in the exact same place the tree always goes. Then Mom and Emma and I decorate the tree. Dad does his usual job, which is to sit in his chair, read the paper, and every once in a while look up to tell us where there's a blank spot on the tree that needs an ornament.

One of the things I like a lot is coming downstairs the morning after we put up our tree. I stop partway down the steps and look into the living room at the tree, with the sun shining on all the decorations. When I was a little kid, this would always be a big surprise because they wouldn't start decorating until I was in bed. I'd see the blank green tree before I went to bed, and then in the morning I'd see a magical, colorful tree, sparkling and twinkling in the sunlight. If I concentrate for a second, I can get just about the same excited, surprised feeling, even though I saw the whole tree decorated last night.

After breakfast I decide to call Leo.

Caroline answers the phone in this sweet little-girl voice.

"Hey, Caroline! It's Emily! How are you?" My voice is overly enthusiastic, which I hate because kids always pick up on that. But right now I can't stop myself. "Did you write your letter to Santa?"

"No."

"No? Oh, well, I sure did!" The exaggerated enthusiasm's making me practically gag. "How else will Santa know what to bring on Christmas Eve?"

There's silence on the other end of the phone.

To let her off the hook, I say, "I guess Santa just knows stuff like that."

But Caroline's on another train of thought. "Leo's girlfriend is Sam."

I'm not sure if I'm supposed to take this as a bit of gossip or a warning to lay off calling him. "Sam's a real nice person. She plays an awesome flute," I say, just to underline the fact that there's no competition between Sam and me.

More silence.

Time to move on. "Is Leo there right now?"

"Sam's here."

"Hey, that's cool!"

Then I hear Leo's voice in the background and Caroline tells him it's me calling.

"I wondered who she was spilling the beans to," he says. "What's up?"

"Nothing. Just wanted to call."

"Is your complicated life worked out yet?"

"A bit. Are things sort of okay with you right now?"

"Gettin' there."

"I'm glad Sam's with you."

"Yeah." He gives a little laugh. "She's got Caroline playing the flute. 'Three Blind Mice.' When she finishes, she wants to play it again. It'll soon drive us all nuts."

I like the way he sounds. Relaxed. Not totally relaxed, but getting there, like he just said.

"I met this guy. Jacob. I don't really know much about him yet. He seems nice, though." I don't say I've been thinking I might go to Jacob's place next week sometime and just say hi when things feel more calmed down. "Hey! Maybe you and Sam and—"

"Not likely."

·"You didn't even give me a chance to say it."

"Shortcut to the obvious."

Who'm I kidding? As if Leo'd want to double-date with anyone. All of a sudden I get this lost, kind of empty feeling, like somehow my friendship with Leo isn't really going to keep happening. "Leo, you have to promise me something."

"Not really," he says in his usual matter-of-fact way.

"You do! You have to—" I stop. Because he's right. He doesn't have to promise anything. But I do. I need this promise for me. "Leo, I'm going to keep calling you. It's important to me. Really important. And I'm going to keep coming to see you. And Sam and Caroline and Jane and Dan."

"Sure. Why not?" I might be kidding myself, but I think he sounds a bit glad about what I just said. Maybe even more than a bit glad.

When I wake up, I think it's the middle of the night, but I look at my clock and it's just about morning. I get out of bed and get dressed. I go quietly downstairs and stop for a second to look into the dark living room. There's a few tiny sparkles on the tree where light from the streetlight is squeezing in through the blinds.

I bundle up in my winter jacket and scarf and mitts, because for sure it's going to be cold out. I very quietly open the door and close it in slow motion. My plan is to walk down past my old elementary school, along one of the quiet streets, and then down toward the harbor, where there's a small park and you can walk up a path to the top of the hill.

By the time I get to the park, it's not really dark anymore. There's pale blue light coming out of nowhere and starting to fill up the sky. When I get all the way to the top of the path, I can see over the trees and houses and across the harbor to the city and hills on the other side.

It's barely morning, and I can hear traffic noises already building up. Everyone's starting to do whatever they always do every single day.

Like it all makes sense and there are no surprises.

Questions for Discussion

* In Chapter One, Emily seems to be more affected by the loss of her boyfriend than she is by the death of her grandfather. How else does she reveal her character at the beginning of the story?

* When Emily cuts up the photos taken of her and Brian, why does she keep the scraps where she appears instead of just throwing them away?

* Why do you think Emily chose not to tell her family about her breakup with Brian right away? And what do you think about her timing when she does decide to tell her parents?

* Why do you think Emily is so attached to Meredith?

* Emily doesn't seem that impressed with Ronny, so why does she ditch the party to go home with him?

* At first glance, Leo seems like a bad bet as a friend, and he makes it clear to Emily that she is not his type. Why do you think Emily gravitates toward him anyway?

* Jenn has been Emily's best friend since they were in grade school, but would you describe them as close friends now? How do you think high school has changed their relationship?

* Leo describes *Romeo and Juliet* as "crap" and Shakespeare as "a pervert." But what does Leo's musical score reveal about his connection to the play?

* When Leo drives off in his father's truck and leaves it with the keys inside and the motor running, he says he is doing it "because it'll piss my father off when he eventually finds his precious truck." What else do you think the gesture says about Leo's view of his father?

* What do you think of Emily's decision to send Brian a card with her cut-up pictures inside?

* Why do you think that Leo immediately falls for Sam?

* The death of Emily's grandfather reveals a number of family secrets, culminating in the discovery of Emily's birth mother. Would Emily have been better off not knowing any of these secrets?

* Why is Emily not upset when Jenn ditches her to go off with her new boyfriend?

* Emily meets Jacob when she is at her most vulnerable, yet she rejects his advances. What does it say about her growth as a character? And do you think she has really seen the last of Jacob?

* At what point in the story would you say that Emily and Leo become genuine friends?

* Mr. Canning asks the students to come up with a theme song for Act One of *Romeo and Juliet*. What theme song would you have chosen for the first — and last — chapters of *Emily for Real*?

* Why do you think the author called this story *Emily for Real*?

Sylvia Gunnery is the author of many books for teens and younger readers. Throughout her teaching career, she has been inspired by her students to create authentic and engaging stories. *Out of Bounds*, the first in her series of sports novels, is a Best Books for Kids and Teens/Our Choice Selection and was nominated for the Hackmatack Children's Choice Book Award. Sylvia gives writing workshops in her home province of Nova Scotia and across Canada, encouraging young writers to find their own voices and tell their own stories.